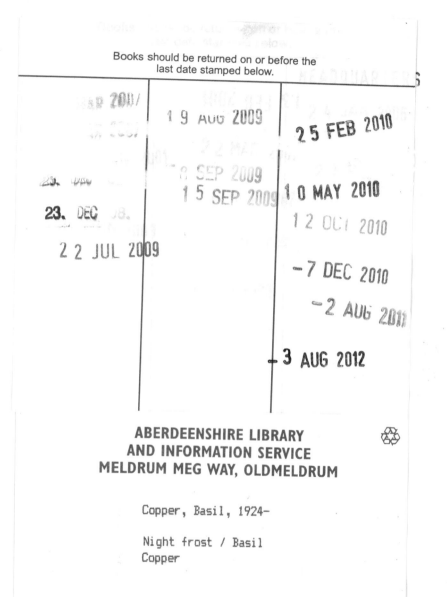

B

NIGHT FROST

American private investigator Mike Faraday is on holiday in the beautiful Bahamas. There's not much rest for him however, after he sees a body being dumped on a beach and he quickly becomes involved in the violent Mafia underworld.

There's never a dull moment in this story, and Mike takes a few batterings along the way. Throughout the book our main man shows his own brand of humour and it's obvious that Mike is a red-blooded male who appreciates the female form.

NIGHT FROST

Basil Copper

·BLACK·
DAGGER
·CRIME·

First published 1966
by
Robert Hale Ltd

This edition 2000 by Chivers Press
published by arrangement with
the author

ISBN 0 7540 8574 0

British Library Cataloguing in Publication Data available

POUR MARIE-ANTOINETTE GUERIN
—MAMAN—

Printed and bound in Great Britain by
Redwood Books, Trowbridge, Wiltshire

CONTENTS

CHAPTER ONE

A Drink for Colonel Clay

I

I SAT BACK in a cane chair, finished off the tall drink in the ice-cold glass and adjusted my straw hat to a finer angle over my eyes. This was as good as it was ever likely to be, I reflected, peeking at white sand, combing green and white sea and striped sunshades, from beneath my lowered lids. Stella and I had come out for a short vacation that had already lengthened to two weeks. I had got a hire car in Tallahassie and we drove down the Cays, mostly admiring the scenery and loafing here and there, wherever the fancy took us.

I hadn't left any forwarding address and put out of my mind the pile of bills that might be mounting up on the mat of my L.A. office. It was Stella who had persuaded us to come on over to the Bahamas. Neither of us had wanted to see the worn-out commercialism of Cape Kennedy, so we skipped out of the U.S. on one of the island short-hop airline companies and set down at Nassau. This was too crowded so we came on down the islands until we got to this place.

There was a plane only about every three days and it

suited us, so it was likely we would finish off the vacation here. I didn't know whether I'd be in any hurry to move even then. A usually impecunious P.I. like me takes easily to unaccustomed leisure and Uncle Sam had been more than generous over my last case.* Way things were going I could loaf on till the fall.

I opened my eyes again as a blonde number, her hair bleached almost white with sun, went by in a polka dot bikini that wouldn't have covered up a self-respecting squirrel. I hastily closed my eyes again. It was hot enough as it was. Hell, I thought to myself, I could stay on until fall next year at this rate.

Even the squeal of a transistor radio from the tiled terrace over by the marble swim pool couldn't spoil my pleasure. Why they had to have a swim pool a few yards from the edge of the sea, I didn't know. It was that kind of place. I closed my eyes again as a tall, coloured waiter in a scarlet jacket and white drill trousers carried another clinking tray of tall iced drinks out to the group next to where I was sitting. The sun was so strong that his shadow etched itself heavily over my closed eyelids.

Everyone looked contented down here. Too contented in fact, but I didn't blame them. The island was surrounded by a sea that shaded off from deepest blue to green and then to bright yellow where the bottom shallowed to sand. It was only about twelve by eight, but it had a small town, three or four villages, a dozen or so clubs and hotels and even an airstrip. The brochures said nothing about poisonous snakes or insects, but even so it would do until the Pearly Gates loomed up.

Stella had gone off shopping somewhere so I had a couple of hours free time until lunch. I was employing them the best way I knew how. Semi-prostrate and semi-comatose. It was the rule of the islands. Half an hour later I woke up conscious that I was beginning to grill;

* See *The Dark Mirror*

sweat was dripping off me and soaking in the cane chair which was starting to stripe my back. Time I got moving.

I went down the beach at a run which must have seemed suicidal to the natives in this climate. I hit the sea in a shallow dive, was knocked under by the big comber which followed and came up spluttering and full of salt water. It was good, though the temperature of the sea was like warm milk. The girl in the bikini came down to the water's edge and made a perfect dive; she didn't wear a bathing cap and she didn't need one.

She came up looking as though she had spent three hours in a beauty salon, creamed through the water in a perfect overarm crawl and passed me doing about sixty knots, effortlessly heading out to sea. She gave me a dazzing smile. I tried to give her a casual wave in reply and went to the bottom again. When I surfaced trying to look as though it was intentional, the fast number was half-way to Nassau. I sighed and trod water. I guessed I'd stay inshore and paddle. It was probably safer.

I horsed around in the water for another twenty minutes and then gave up; it was too hot, even in there. When I came out and went up the beach to dry off, one of the waiters in the scarlet coats came hurrying down from the hotel terrace. He met me just as I was making the third pass with the towel over my body; I didn't need anything more. I was dry by then anyway, in this climate.

" Telephone, sir," said the redcoat. I guess I must have looked surprised.

" I'm hardly dressed . . ." I said.

He gave me a pepsodent smile. " That's all right, sir. I've brought it out on the terrace."

When I got back to my chair there was a mile of white cable leading to a junction box in the hotel patio. The telephone itself, in a rather neat arrangement, was hooked over the back of the chair. It was Stella.

" Sorry to trouble you, Mike."

" A pleasure," I said.

" Are you doing anything?" she asked.

" Not so's you'd notice," I said. " Get to the point, sweetie."

" I wondered if you could run out and pick me up," she said. " I'm at Conch Cay. Mrs. McSwayne ran me over to do some shopping and intended to bring me back, but she met some friends and is staying on for a drink. You sure you don't mind?"

" Not at all," I said insincerely. " Be right out."

Mrs. McSwayne was the wife of the proprietor of our hotel and Conch Cay was the nearest village of any size; it was about four miles to the north, but it seemed about the same distance as Zululand in this heat. I looked at the sea again and sighed heavily. Why these women had to go shopping at all on holiday beat me, especially when there was a small shop in the hotel. But there it was.

2

I put on a blue silk sports shirt over my bathing trunks, scuffed on some sandals and I was ready. I took my hire car keys out of my trousers pocket and left the rest of my stuff on the chair. I had some paper money in the pocket of my shirt. On the way out I asked the porter to keep an eye on my things. I hadn't left any money and this might be British soil and all that, but I've had property stolen in better places than this. When I drove around front a couple of minutes later I saw the porter carrying my stuff inside.

I'd hired a Caddy, despite my misgivings, but Stella had so many cases of junk she wanted to bring with her, I figured it was easier to throw everything on the back seat. We used a coupon system from the hire firm, which meant we had an identical Caddy waiting for us wherever we stopped off; on islands where they had cars, that is. We hadn't bothered in Nassau but a car would help on a place like this; and there would be another waiting for us back in Florida.

Good as the service was I preferred my old Buick and on these narrow roads it didn't seem possible for any other car to get past us; so far they had, but I'd got my doubts, just the same. There was a little breeze up here on the point as the big black car drifted round the dusty roads hacked out of the solid rock. Lush vegetation brushed against the windows as I slowed to let a yellow station waggon go by; the coloured woman driving it gave me a smile like a sunburst.

As I picked up speed again, a bunch of scarlet flowers cut off by the edge of the open window landed on my lap. I figured I could drive with one hand and pick bananas with the other. Conch Cay was a sliver of dazzling white houses and shops, strung round a half-moon of emerald water where fishing boats and yachts danced at anchor in a lazy swell. I brought the Caddy to a gentle halt in a feathering of white dust from the roadway. I got out of the driving seat like an old man of eighty with rheumatism. The heat here made L.A. seem like Alaska, and I didn't aim to bust a gut in this atmosphere.

I nodded to a dark-skinned gentleman whose Palm Beach tan made his face almost invisible. I couldn't see Stella anywhere around so I went into the Bonefish Inn. Ceiling fans redistributed the hot air and it was only minutely cooler than outside, but even that was something. The floor seemed to be made of black glass, there was a lot of cane furniture, cane blinds, cane shutters at the big windows; they were all latched back now to catch what breeze there was off the sea.

There were quite a few people in the cocktail lounge; a high-voiced blonde woman in a yellow beach outfit which

emphasised her Michelin-tyre mid-riff, a party of visiting
Rotarians, a few over-hearty Colonial-type Englishmen,
an obvious bar-fly or two. The two white-coated
Bahamians at the bar seemed to be busy, so I sat down
in a corner and studied the company. While I was doing
this a big man in a pearl-grey suit drifted in.

He wore a white panama, yellow socks and beach
shoes. He got immediate attention from the bar-tenders.
I guessed it was on account of his size. He was about
nine feet tall and broad with it. I figured he'd at least
ask for a double paraffin but he settled for a whisky. I
felt disappointed. I caught the bar-tender's eye so I edged
up behind Carnera. I felt like a dinghy alongside a battleship.

" What'll be your pleasure, sah?" the bar-keep said in
that well-modulated low voice they all have in the islands.
It's supposed to sound very English, but I didn't find it
hard to take. I ordered a lime-juice with a dash of something hard in it and plenty of ice. I carried the clinking
glass over to one of the big windows and sat sipping and
looking out over the blue stretch of sea and sky. This was
one of the better days in a P.I.'s life, I decided.

I had been there about fifteen minutes, thinking about
nothing in particular and absorbing local colour, when
I saw Stella pass the window. She was with some other
people, but I guessed she'd see the car and come on in.
I just had time to order a drink for her and sit down again
before a group of people came in through the outer door.
There were Stella, a middle-aged couple I recognised as
Mr. and Mrs. McSwayne and a tallish, military-looking
figure in a grey flannel suit I hadn't seen before.

Stella detached herself and came on over.

" Hi," she said. I made a suitably inane reply. Stella's
been my secretary for some while now, but I couldn't
get used to seeing her like this. She wore sky-blue shorts that
fitted her body like she'd grown up inside them, a matching

shirt-top that left four inches of bronzed mid-riff bare, and her long, lazy legs ended up in white cork and leather beach shoes. She had all the usual accessories but it was the way they were distributed on her that kept me interested. Apart from that she was just about the best secretary in the business.

I finished making my inventory and realising it was too hot, I raised my eyes to her face. She wore an amused look, like she knew what I was thinking, which she probably guessed anyway. Her honey-blonde hair was drawn back with a blue ribbon the same colour as her outfit. The coloured bar-tender risked a heat stroke with the rate he trundled Stella's long drink over. I noticed he didn't provide the same facilities for the other people in the bar. But I didn't blame him for that.

"Come over to the bar, Mike," Stella said. "There's someone I'd like you to meet."

We left our drinks on the table. The McSwaynes greeted me with noisy effusiveness and then moved off down the bar to join their friends. The man in the grey flannel suit had just picked up a whisky as we came up behind him. He was around sixty, I should have guessed, well-preserved, with a wiry frame. His tan was deep and even, his grey hair brushed impeccably back from the temples. His grey eyes were clear and a small white mustache was carefully trimmed back from his lips. Even without the regimental tie neatly tucked in under his cream shirt tabs he had British officer stamped all over him.

"This is Colonel Clay," said Stella, introducing me.

The Colonel smiled. His grip was dry and firm. "Delighted," he said in that clipped voice which annoys some Americans, but which I find curiously attractive. "Delighted, Mr. Faraday; I've been wanting to meet you. Didn't I read something about that Washington business, the other day? Afraid you'll find it very dull down here. Not much like your line of country."

" Suits me," I said. " We're on vacation."

" So the little lady told me," he said. " I'm in the same line of business myself."

" Oh," I said.

" Colonel Clay represents the British Government in these parts," said Stella, deftly steering the three of us back to our table.

The Colonel shrugged deprecatingly. " I'd hardly put it like that," he said. " Bit of diplomacy, bit of police work, you know the sort of thing."

He drank from his glass. " For my sins," he added, in the short silence which followed. " You must both come to dinner with me, one evening—if you're staying, that is."

" We'd like to," I said. I was partly turned towards the door of the bar and I was studying the big man, who had turned back to the bar-keep for another drink and was now engaging him in conversation. I noticed he kept his eye on the big clock over the main door of the bar. There was something about him which seemed vaguely familiar, but I couldn't place it.

" I was just telling the little lady," the Colonel was saying, " there's a regatta and military parade over here on Saturday. Should be worth watching. They've got a Highland Regiment coming over. Though perhaps that sort of British function bores you, Mr. Faraday? Bit pompous for some Americans, I daresay?"

" I can take it or leave it," I said. " I've got nothing against England, if that's what you mean."

He laughed. " Quite so," he said. " I didn't mean to put it like that."

We talked on for another ten minutes and then he looked at the discreet gold watch at his wrist and said he had to go. He was an engaging old buffer and it had been quite an entertaining quarter of an hour. We all got up together and I promised to take him up on the dinner engagement. He said he'd give us a ring at the hotel.

We all went out of the bar door in a bunch, waving to the McSwaynes over in the corner. Stella picked up a big cane shopping basket from the bar-tender and gave it to me to carry. I might have made some comment but we had the Colonel with us. As we came out the door, I nearly cannoned into a little man who was hurrying up the steps. He wore a bright red T-shirt; all I could see clearly of his face was a bald patch on his forehead and a pair of mean, close-set eyes, but it was enough. He muttered an apology with ill grace and went inside, his eyes raking the room.

I stood on the steps for a moment, letting Stella and the Colonel get ahead. I saw red-shirt go up to the big gorilla at the bar and start talking excitedly to him. Then they shifted over to a table in the middle of the room. I went on down the steps and joined the Colonel and Stella. He was sitting at the wheel of a scarlet Alvis, a little English sports job, that looked ideal for these narrow roads with its small build and rakish lines. I noticed he wore wash-leather gloves for driving, even in this heat.

" It's been a pleasure, Mr. Faraday," he said to me with a smile. " We really must make that a definite evening."

He lit a cigarette with a gold motif stencilled on it from a lighter set into the car dashboard. I was disappointed. I thought he was going to get a Meerschaum pipe and a deer-stalker from the glove-locker. He nodded again, gave Stella a long smile of appreciation and was off, the car sliding smoothly from the lot onto the road, with an imperceptible gear-change. He didn't rev the engine or accentuate the gears and I should have said he was quite a driver. In a second or two he was a scarlet dot in the middle of a dust cloud.

" I bet he was a boy when he was about twenty-five," I said reflectively.

" He isn't so bad now," said Stella with definite appreciation.

"Don't be disgusting," I told her puritanically. She chuckled.

We went over to the Caddy. I winced as I eased myself into the driving seat and slung Stella's basket in the back. The heat of the leather seat seared its way through my thin shirt and raised the perspiration on my bare legs. Stella just sat down and fussed with her handbag. She didn't seem to notice the heat at all and I noticed there wasn't a bead of perspiration on her forehead.

I sat on for a few seconds longer, puzzling out something. I looked back at the Inn. The two men who occupied my thoughts were now sitting at the window. I fancied they were looking over in our direction.

"Penny for them," said Stella, frowning at my concentration.

I didn't answer for a moment. Then I started the motor and gunned the car smoothly out of the lot.

"I was just wondering," I said. "Wondering what a Chicago mobster was doing in a place like this."

I still hadn't got the answer by the time we arrived back at the hotel.

CHAPTER TWO

On the Beach

I

THE LUNCH was specially good. Stella and I sat on in the dining-room and worked our way through a second helping of coconut-tomato soup, followed by guava chutney. I settled for baked plantains with minced beef as a follow-up and lolled forward in my chair, one hand on the stem of an agreeably chilled glass. I sat with my back to the sea; somehow I had enough of the blue stuff for one morning, but Stella looked eagerly out through the window over my shoulder as though she was afraid of missing something.

It was difficult to spoil that girl's enthusiasm, I told myself Hell, though, she had earned a holiday just as I had. She had changed into a lemon-yellow dress, with a pink scarf at her neck; the top two buttons of the dress were open but the modest cleavage revealed generated as much interest in me as it would have if another woman's had been open down to the navel. I really would have to do something about Stella some time, I told myself. Right now it was too hot. I took a mental reservation for the winter months and went back to the menu.

"Where did you meet the Colonel?" I said, returning to a topic we had touched on earlier. Stella frowned slightly and waved offhandedly to a shadow passing the window outside the dining-room.

"Somewhere in Conch Cay, I suppose," she said. "He suddenly seemed to be there. He's that sort of man. The McSwaynes said something about him coming to see his boat. He keeps a small yacht there. Supposed to be very fond of fishing. So it seemed natural to ask him to join us for a drink."

She wrinkled her nose. "Why the inquisition, chum?"

I laughed. "Don't flatter yourself," I said. "I'm not jealous. It was just that I was curious about the Colonel. I wondered how much of his interest was social, and how much professional."

Light dawned on Stella's face. She smiled faintly.

"You mean the two men at the Inn?" she asked.

"Could be," I said. "One of them at least has a criminal record. I wonder whether I ought to mention it to the old boy when he rings."

"For Pete's sake, Mike, let it rest," said Stella. "After all, you are on holiday."

"Just idle curiosity," I reassured her. "I don't want to get mixed up in international affairs. British territory, don't yer know."

She laughed at my imitation of the English accent as the waiter appeared again at my elbow. We ordered dessert and a *demi-tasse* to follow.

Though it was as hot as all hell, we just couldn't keep off the coffee.

"All the same, sweetie," I said, draining my second cup a few minutes later, "a word in the Colonel's ear wouldn't come amiss."

She frowned again but said nothing.

"All well, sah?" said the waiter, materialising from somewhere behind my right shoulder. I might have jumped except that I was too well-trained. All the same he would have made a good professional assassin.

" First-rate," I reassured him. He grinned from ear to ear.

I figured the recommendation would cost me at least another dollar on the tip.

As we went down the terrace after the meal I stopped and looked towards the beach. There was a familiar figure playing with a black and white striped rubber ball. Her legs were etched black against the liquid silver of the sea but there came a flash of gold as she changed position and the sun caught her hair. Then she ran farther up the beach and I saw once again the polka-dot bikini that had caught my attention in the morning.

I glanced towards Stella but she had gone back up the terrace towards the hotel lobby. The blonde number spun on one leg and struck a pose against the ocean backdrop. Then she waved cheekily to me. I waved too. She threw the ball towards me and waited. It was pretty obvious she wanted me to throw it back. I pointed towards the receding figure of Stella and shrugged. I could see her grin even from that distance.

I went on into the hotel lobby. On pretext of smelling the flowers on an ornamental table set into the wall on one side of the tesselated pavement, I glanced into the gilt mirror meant to double the effect of the flowers. I thought I looked pretty trim, seeing I was in my thirties and all. All right, Faraday, I said to myself; you've still got it, boy.

Stella's humorous cough sounded right behind me, but her smooth face remained enigmatic in the mirror. But I could have sworn she knew what I was thinking. I followed her up the stairs laughing to myself.

2

In the afternoon Stella went to lie down for an hour or
two. I horsed around in the water for a bit. I was still
thinking about the two men at the Bonefish Inn, and the
exercise and the salt spray cleared my brain and what
with the sun and the sea and a swell which had blown up
it eventually went out of my mind. The water seemed
even warmer than the morning; I borrowed a snorkel
from the loan equipment stall in the hotel lobby and
amused myself for an hour or two studying the fish.

There was a little red and white striped number that
seemed to have taken quite a shine to me, and he stayed
with me for more than half an hour, until I shook him off
among the coral. I came to the conclusion that I wasn't
really cut out for this; I can swim pretty well so far as
stamina and determination are concerned. I guess my
range is about two miles, but I lack style and the crawl
has never really been my type of thing. I can't keep it up
long enough and the trick of it has always evaded me.

I was just about tired of scrabbling about the coral
and chasing fish which were never there, when something
pink flashed across my field of view. I had on goggles, of
course, as well as the snorkel tube and what with the
flippers and all I was far from a figure of grace. So I took
some while to adjust and while I was struggling to look
back over my shoulder whatever it was had gone. I surfaced for air and when I went back down again, a shadow
flitted across the striped bands of sun which went dancing
through the water.

I followed on down behind a waving belt of weed and
saw something dappled slide away behind the pink and
yellow coral. I followed again but whatever it was was
making pretty good time and it wasn't going to wait

around for me. By the time I got there, a swirl in the water and a few bubbles formed the only trace.

I trod water. I wasn't really thinking of danger or anything like that; my mind was on fish, but I shuddered more than somewhat when something caught my right ankle way down in the depths of the weed. It was a light but strong touch and as I went downwards, I was too surprised to react. Then the grip was relaxed and as I floated face downwards, something sharp and playful tickled the soles of my feet.

As I corkscrewed to the surface, the speckled shape went swirling up past me at terrific speed. I saw something like long strands of yellow water weed and spots danced before my eyes. As the shape passed within two feet of my face something waved almost derisively. I saw five small toes gleaming with pink nail varnish as the blonde job in the polka-dot bikini creamed her way effortlessly to the surface. It's difficult under water, I know, but I could have sworn she was laughing.

When I broke water about half an hour afterwards she was just a splash of white, tumbled surf, almost inshore. I got to a raft anchored off the beach and flopped down to take off my gear. The sun was as keen as a knife blade up here. As I sat up and dashed the water from my hair, the blonde job stood up in the water at the edge of the beach. She waved and disappeared among the beach umbrellas with a long, athletic stride.

I didn't bother to reply to her salutation. She couldn't see me anyway. But I looked long and carefully at the place where she'd disappeared. I'm no Tristan but she sure looked like Isolde, or something around that price-range.

I'd brought my cigarettes and lighter in a water-proof purse I'd stashed in a pocket of my trunks and I smoked and sunned myself for a bit before heading in to the beach. I thought about the blonde number and the two guys at the Inn, and Stella and Colonel Clay and a hundred other things that don't concern the story.

Then, because the whole thing seemed a footling waste of time, I pitched the stub of my cigarette overboard, shifted over on to my face and dozed for a while. The slap, slap of the water hitting the edge of the raft dulled my senses and made a pleasant background, and the harsh, antiseptic rinse of the sun on my body was real good. I felt the coolness of the wet matting under my body and then I slept.

When I woke it was still hot but the best of the afternoon was gone. There were long, blue shadows on the beach and on the white, rocky hills that bordered the shore and a breeze had sprung up. I went off the raft in a long shallow dive, holding the snorkel kit in one hand and when I came up I amused myself by swimming face downwards, just under the surface of the water. The sea still retained the heat of the day and I was sorry that I only got around to this sort of thing about once every five years. A weekend at Santa Monica was more like my line, and then I usually ended up playing the horses.

When I got up the beach there was no sign of the blonde job or Stella, so I sat in a cane chair and smoked another cigarette and then went on up to my room. The plan for the guest apartments at the Catamaran was rather unusual; they ran up three or four flights, the rooms opening off spacious corridors. The apartments were built around a square, open to the sky at the top, something on the lines of an Elizabethan inn, and down below was a courtyard with multi-coloured flowers and a fountain playing in the middle. Shades of Old Seville and all that sort of stuff. But very nice, if you like that sort of thing.

I did and I stood on the balcony on my floor for a bit, finished my cigarette and just drank in the atmosphere. Stella's room was a couple of doors down from mine and I debated whether to give her a tap, but decided to let her sleep on. There was no real reason for my disturbing her and she might be taking a bath or something.

Just before I went in to my room, I flicked my cigarette butt down into the basin of the fountain. Awfully bad form and all that, but I couldn't entirely shake my bad manners of L.A. and the cigarette had left my hand before I gave it another thought. It described a fiery parabola in the air and shot a stream of sparks as it hit the fountain basin and bounced off into the water.

There was a scuttering in the foliage nearby as the sparks seemed to disturb somebody in the shadow, and a form in a grubby white drill suit hurried out into the centre of the courtyard. " Sorry," I called down after him. Normally I don't go in for that sort of refinement, but I was on holiday and courtesy costs nothing, like they say. He didn't answer but went on up the staircase opposite. The plan of the hotel was such that anyone on the upper floors had to make the entire circuit of the corridors for the next flight so I stayed put.

Just idle curiosity, but I had nothing else to do, so I thought I'd see who he was. The figure came on round the flight below me and presently appeared again opposite, at the same level I was standing. He started off on another circuit and as he neared me, I saw he was a tall, spare-shouldered character with a crumpled red neck-tie. He looked unshaven and dirty, which was unusual for this class of hotel. He gave me an odd, haunted look from the corner of his eyes as he went by.

I watched him off; he turned his head once and then mopped at his neck with a far from clean handkerchief. He went up on to the third floor—the one above me—and presently I heard a door softly close in the silence. I shrugged and went on into my own room. I saw enough of nut-cases in L.A. without cultivating them on holiday.

3

When I came down to dinner the heat of the day had fined off to what was termed cool in this part of the world. It was no longer roasting, just sweltering. But the big fans in the dining-room were hard at work and with the windows open and a breeze coming off the sea I felt I might get through the evening. I went on into the main bar while I waited for Stella.

There was a three piece band playing samba rhythms over in a corner of the dining-room and half a dozen couples working off their excess energy on a pint-sized dance floor. I ordered a gin fizz with plenty of ice and watched the work-out. The blonde job I had seen at the Bonefish Inn in the morning was doing fancy steps with a man old enough to be her father; he had a long horse face, white mustache and silver sideboards. They danced like they were glued together and the expression on their faces wasn't at all filial, so I guessed he wasn't her father at that.

As an exhibition it wasn't up to Vernon and Irene Castle so I turned back to the bar-keep and we chatted about this and that while I filled in time. He had come over from another island for the tourist season; in off periods he earned a living fishing, I gathered. The bar was a pretty elaborate place, though the whole of the Catamaran was lavish, considering it was only a medium-sized lay-out. One wall was taken up with a thirty feet tank filled with tropical fish; the thing was lit with lights which changed colour as the evening progressed.

It was all right early on when you had only one or two drinks but it could be murder when you'd sunk a lot under your belt, the evening was getting on and the lighting had reached the mauve cycle. The women weren't so bad but the men's faces were deadly; it reminded me of the Richmond Street morgue back in L.A. during the high season.

Just then I caught sight of Stella coming down the staircase; she had done something new to her hair and she looked as fresh as the morning. I meant her to join me at the bar but then I changed my mind. In the fish tank behind the bar-tender, elongated and even more massive among the writhing fish forms, I could see reflected a vast, pearl-grey shape that hadn't been there a minute or two before.

I asked a passing waiter to bring a couple of drinks over to our table and went on into the dining-room to meet Stella. The big man in the grey suit—the one nine feet tall who didn't drink paraffin—looked like he might know me, but I didn't want to give him time to make sure. I didn't see him again though and when I looked up half-way through dinner he had left the bar.

Afterwards I got the Caddy and we drove out to the point. We just sat in the car inhaling the fresh scent of wild orchid, orange blossom and all that sort of stuff. In front a moon rode high, slicing the edges of the palms and in front the silver of the Atlantic rode straight out for thousands of miles, its surface fretted and splintered into a million patterns by the soft breath of the Trades.

" Isn't this gorgeous, Mike?" said Stella, her mouth close up against my face.

" Cook's Tours and the world before you," I said, my voice muffled by her hair.

" You're just an old cynic," complained Stella. " But don't think that will spoil my holiday."

It didn't. When we sat up a few minutes later my tie was rumpled, my hair mussed and my nerves tingling all the way down to my socks. I lit a cigarette, thinking it more prudent and got out of the car to stretch my legs.

Stella joined me and we took a turn along the cliff edge.

It wound down along the shore and eventually turned into a steep track leading through the dark shadowed undergrowth and the palms, to a secluded beach where white sand shone brightly even in this light. I thought it might be time to turn back. We stood for a moment looking idly down into the cove.

I had been watching a small boat for the past few minutes, which made its way like a water beetle, a black shadow trailing it, across the surface of the sea. There were two men in it and something seemed familiar about them, even at that distance. As we stood there the boat grounded ashore and the two men got out carrying something between them. There was no doubting what it was, even a quarter of a mile away.

" Stay here," I told Stella.

" Mike, what are you going to do?" she called after me. It was a quiet night and her voice sounded a long way away.

I was already running down the rocky path in the dark and I cursed as I saw the two men look up. They hesitated and then dropped their burden. It sprawled like a dark star-fish at their feet. I zig-zagged through the palms, to come at them the shortest way across the sand, but it was already too late.

As I broke through into the moonlight, the oars grated in the rowlocks and the boat floated free across the surf and into the open sea. I put back my shoulders, dropped my coat and started off at a fast dive across the powdery beach when a light winked from the dark shadow of the boat, something whined off a stone and a great puff of sand spread in a scattering cloud half a dozen feet from me. I went down on to my face and stayed down.

You don't carry Smith-Wessons on vacation and it would have been plain crazy to have tried anything with that sort of opposition. So I stayed put until I judged it was safe to move and when I put my head up I saw they were out of range. I got up then. I could see Stella down at the edge of the trees and she started picking her way towards me, until I waved her back. I waited until I saw she was well up near the car and then turned to see who had been left on the beach.

He was a tall, thin man in a white drill suit. He lay on his face, with his arms spread out, just as he had been dropped. There was no blood, no sign of a wound, but he was quite dead. I turned him over gently. It was my seedy friend with the red tie from the hotel courtyard earlier that afternoon. I can't say why, but I wasn't at all surprised. His face was colder than death and his hands gave off a chill more final than the tomb. I laid him reverently back again and stood up. Something broke off from one of his fingers and I examined it absently in the moonlight.

I looked thoughtfully after the miniscule form of the boat, bobbing among the wavelets, just rounding the point and I knew it would be useless to follow. They would soon be among the yacht anchorage where any one of half a hundred boats could be their destination. And anyway I hadn't seen their faces. I went back up along the cliff and met Stella. She looked anxious.

" We'd better get Colonel Clay," I said. " This is more in his department." I led the way back to the car.

I had to turn it around in the roughness of the narrow road. Stella's face was concerned in the moonlight.

" That was a body, wasn't it?" she said. " What does it all mean?"

" The end of my holiday," I said, setting the car bonnet back towards the Catamaran.

CHAPTER THREE

Night Frost

I

THE NIGHT was alive with people. Up on the road a blaze of headlights illuminated the path down towards the beach. At the edge of the trees a portable generator hummed, feeding a set of powerful arc-lights, their cables trailing like snakes across the white sand, competing with the moon. Up the hill an ambulance, the red cross a vivid splash on its white-painted sides, edged delicately down the path as near as possible to the beach.

Colonel Clay stood frowning in the light of the lamps. I told him my story for the second time. He pulled at his lower lip. A muscular native police sergeant, his khaki drill outfit impeccably creased, passed me on his way up with a message for the doctor. He muttered a soft apology as he brushed against me in the shadow. Two more native constables stood guard on the sheeted form under the arcs.

Up on the road I could hear a patrol car radio spitting out static and instructions into the night. The soft mumble of the surf came to us from far out, advancing and receding under the stars.

"We really can't have this sort of thing," said the Colonel, more to himself than to me, as I finished speaking. "I don't like this on my patch at all." I looked at him sharply; his face gave nothing away, but I could detect a faint edge of humour in his voice. I glanced back at the sheeted figure again.

"It is rather bad form," I said blandly. The Colonel didn't blink or alter the inflexion of his voice by a fraction; a true diplomat, he went smoothly on as though I hadn't interrupted.

"We really ought to get that lass of yours back to the hotel," he ventured. "We may be some time out here— that is, if you don't mind the trouble. It really is most good of you . . . but a man of your experience . . . you know what I mean."

There was a brief silence as he looked at me again. I didn't let him down.

"No trouble," I said. "I'm at your disposal. I was getting a little bit bored with the holiday anyway."

"Right, then," said the Colonel cheerfully. "Let's get up top and sort a few things out."

He turned to the two constables on guard. "Keep your eyes open," he said. "The doctor will be here soon. I'll be up at the radio car for the next twenty minutes if you want me. But one of you must stay here all the time. I don't want him left."

The men saluted smartly as he passed out of the arcs and joined me in the shadow. We went up off the beach.

"I'd better get this sand sifted," he muttered as we stumbled up the path. "It will be difficult to find the bullet but it may be helpful."

He was talking about the bullet which had been fired at me. I'd pointed out the spot roughly, as best I remembered it, working from the position of the body, and he'd already had the area staked out with little flags. I was beginning to see that he was pretty efficient in his Olde

Englishe way. A man in a white drill suit jumped out of the ambulance door as it met us as far down the track as the driver dared to go. He nodded at Clay who introduced him to me.

"This is Doctor Griffith. Michael Faraday—I expect you've heard about him lately."

The doctor grinned as he shook hands. "Glad to know you," he said. "Quite a celebrity."

He glanced down towards the beach. "You seem to have a nose for trouble."

"It follows me around," I said. I liked the look of the doc. He was about forty, with black, close-cropped curly hair and a powerful, open face. He had broad shoulders and walked like an athlete. I found out later he'd been a good all-rounder and an outstanding polo player. A good man in a corner, I figured.

"What's all the panic?" said Griffith.

"There's a man down there," said the Colonel evenly. "I want to find out all about him. He was a sheet of ice when Mr. Faraday here blew across him."

Griffith goggled. "Impossible!" he exploded. He looked from me to Clay and back to me again. "You're kidding?"

I shook my head. "Not only was he as cold as a statue's ass in January but I broke a piece of ice off him."

Griffith's face was a picture.

"There isn't time to go into all that now, Colin," Clay told him curtly. "We'll explain presently. I want you to get down there before he melts entirely and tell us what you think."

Griffith seized his bag from the front seat of the ambulance and set off for the beach at a rush. Two ambulance attendants followed at a more leisurely pace, carrying a stretcher with leather straps. Stella was sitting in the back of the patrol car when we got up to it, listening to the police radio. A constable sat stolidly behind the wheel looking down towards the beach. He looked as bored as all hell.

" Sorry to detain you, my dear," said the Colonel affably. " I think it might be best if I had you driven back to the Catamaran. We're likely to be here half the night."

Stella looked at me helplessly.

" Sorry about this," I told her.

" Don't apologise," she said. I couldn't see her expression in the dark but her voice sounded amused. " And don't try to tell me you aren't enjoying yourself."

" Long vacations aren't really in my line," I said, " and this case does present some interesting problems."

" Like what?" she said.

" Like the corpse being frozen," I said.

" It must be pretty cold in the water this time of night," Stella began. " I can't see what's so unusual."

Colonel Clay chuckled in the darkness and Stella stopped in mid-stride.

" Sorry my dear," he mumbled. " You must forgive my rudeness."

" What the Colonel's trying to say," I said, " is that there's no such thing as frost in the Bahamas. At least there's no such thing recorded in history, either night or day. Even I know that."

" You mugged that up out of the Tourist Guide," said Stella.

" You bet your sweet life I did," I told her. " As it happens, these parties tried to mislead the Colonel here as to the moment of death by quite a few hours. But for the accident of us being at the cove they would have succeeded too. As it is, all they've done is give us a valuable clue as to the place of death. I don't say the place of murder, because we don't yet know how he died."

" I still don't get it," said Stella.

I explained, " The condition of the body means that it must have been refrigerated. That in turn presupposes a plant big enough to take a body, which rules out a domestic refrigerator."

"And there are only a few commercial refrigeration plants on the island fitting those requirements," said the Colonel.

"Which narrows down the search considerably," I finished. I didn't quite do a soft shoe dance in the dust of the trail there, but I felt like it. And I must have looked like it too, for Stella gave a little ironic clap as we stopped talking.

"All right, boys," she said. "I'm on my way. See you in the morning."

I put my head in at the window and kissed her good-night.

"Where does that get you?" she asked as the patrol car motor purred into life. She was referring to our theory, not the kiss.

"We don't know yet," I said. "But it might make all the difference to someone about establishing an alibi."

"Not a bad guess," she said out of the retreating car. "Have fun."

Colonel Clay looked after her admiringly. "A delightful young woman," he said. "May I congratulate you on your good taste."

"She's an excellent secretary, too," I said. He looked at me and coughed suddenly.

"Quite so. Shall we join the doctor?"

I could see he was busy under the light of the arcs, so we loafed down the path to the cove.

"If this is murder, and it certainly looks like it, the refrigeration idea must be important to someone as an alibi," I said. "I saw this party back in the hotel courtyard this afternoon. That was around four. Give or take an hour or so, it's reasonable to suppose he was alive until about half-four—leastways he was still breathing when I saw him. It was around midnight when he was dumped in the cove.

That leaves an interval of at least seven hours—he could have been anywhere or seen anyone in that time."

The Colonel moodily scuffed the toe of his shoe in the sand and kicked idle patterns in its surface. Way over to the right several constables were sifting the sand in large wire meshes under a couple more arc lamps which had been set up to cover the area round the flags.

" This is a small island," he said, " but there's a big visiting population in the hotels and particularly in the yachts which call daily. It will be an easy matter to trace our friend from his hotel registration—in fact it's being done at this minute—but the two men you saw could be anywhere right now. That won't be so easy. However, I've alerted the harbour authorities and the coastguard and all shipping movements have been stopped until we've been through everybody's credentials. Not a dinghy will be going out until we've checked."

I looked at him with more respect. He lowered his voice as an ambulance man passed us carrying a pile of blankets and added, " You say you've got a theory about these two men in the rowing boat?"

" Nothing so strong as that," I said. " Let's just call it a hunch. When you left us at the Bonefish yesterday I thought I recognised a former Chicago mobster in a man that came into the bar. He met another character in there—a big fellow more than six feet tall. I couldn't swear to it, but the couple in the row-boat looked very much like them, though it was hard to make out in the available light. If I were in charge of this case that's where I'd start looking."

He nodded. " I'll get on to that just as soon as I get back to the office," he said.

I had a sudden thought. " You're vetting the air passengers?"

" Surely," he answered. " There isn't another flight out for two days. But all the booking reservations will come to me first."

B

I mentally gave him another high rating.

"No sense in alarming these birds unnecessarily," I said. "I've got a chum in the Chicago police. I could make a few discreet inquiries by phone for you—at the Government's expense," I added.

He smiled thinly. "I think we can go along on that," he said. "Thank you very much, Michael."

It was the first time he had used my Christian name. I thought it was quite an accolade coming from him.

"I'll get on to that early tomorrow morning," I said. "In the meantime what's the drill out here? Have you got enough facilities for handling a large-scale murder hunt?"

He looked at me from under dark brows. "Are you interested in giving us a hand? Is that what you mean? There'd be nothing in it for you—in the way of fees, that is."

I laughed. I didn't feel at all insulted. "My holiday's on the U.S. Government and I've got all the time in the world if you'd like to have me."

He pondered a moment. "You understand I'm really only an amateur policeman. Diplomacy and government in the out-islands are really my line. My correct procedure is to call the experts in from Nassau."

He looked past the doctor and the arc-lamps and the toiling constables out to where the moon's reflection was broken into a billion fragments by the ceaseless motion of the sea.

"I'll have to radio them a report later tonight," he said softly. "But I think we can handle it by ourselves if you're game."

He turned back to me and held out his hand. "To hell with Nassau!" he said. "We don't want to overstrain their resources."

We stood and watched the doctor. He put back the canvas over the dead face and straightened himself.

" I'm going to wash up," he said. " Come along if you like and we'll talk."

The three of us set out down the beach to where the moon-shimmer on the water met the land.

Griffith was silent for a moment. Then he said, " Damned ingenious, you know. I see what you were driving at back there."

" All right, doc," said Colonel Clay. " What did you find?"

" He'd been refrigerated right enough," said Griffith, striding out so that the Colonel had to lengthen his pace to keep up.

" And if he hadn't been found until morning the sun and natural corruption would have removed all trace."

" Interesting," grunted Clay, " but was it murder, man?"

" Sorry," said Griffith. " I was so damned fascinated with the idea that I almost forgot your end. No doubt about it. He'd been killed by a small splinter of ice fired direct into the heart. The entry wound was so small, we might well have overlooked this aspect once corruption set in."

The Colonel's jaw dropped. We had reached the frothing whiteness of the surf now and it was loud in our ears. Griffith dropped to one knee and washed his hands in the sea. He took soap and a small scrub brush from his pocket and briskly scoured his finger nails.

" It's, an old trick," I said. " The ice melts of course, leaving little trace. Verdict; heart failure. And with the refrigeration period not taken into account, it would have confused the issue still further. Time of death might have been estimated at two o'clock this morning. Instead of, as it may well be, around six last evening."

" Not bad," said Griffith, standing up and waving his hands about to dry them in the warm air. " I put it at around seven."

" Emulating your secretary, I'm afraid I don't quite get

this," said Colonel Clay as we started to walk back across the beach to where the arcs made a white splash in the darkness.

" Simple, really," I said, " when you follow out the line of reasoning all the way. Refrigeration—the confusion of time to create an alibi. The splinter of ice—an old gag in lethal circles. Fired by air pressure from a special type of gun. A gun used in killing cattle. Cattle are also killed and refrigerated in deep-freeze plants. And Chicago. The stock-yards, the meat slaughtering centre of the world. Incidentally, the place at least one of the men comes from."

The Colonel looked at me in amazement and his steps suddenly became tottery.

" Good God above, and I thought the Americans were dumb," he muttered. " I can see that your reputation hasn't been exaggerated."

" I don't know whether to be insulted or flattered," I told him. " One or two of us have been known to solve a crime now and again."

Griffith burst out laughing and Colonel Clay joined in. " I'm sorry, Michael," he said, grasping my arm. " But between us I think we're going to have this business sorted out within the next twenty-four hours."

" I've heard that before," I warned him, " but you may have a point there."

We had now reached the spot where the constables were working. The body had been removed to the ambulance and we could see it reversing slowly and jerkily up the beach path. Constables were already removing the main arcs. Three men patiently sifted through tons of sand looking for that elusive bullet.

" We still haven't followed this business right through," I reminded the Colonel. " Leaving aside the identity of the corpse or the fact that the killers may be Chicago professionals, we've got three big leads. The place of death, which shouldn't be too hard to find on a small island like this; the time factor and the alibi, which may pinpoint someone to whom the extra hours may have been important. And the most interesting speculation to me, where were they taking him when Stella and I happened along? He may not have been found for some days if they had dumped him in a house or a beach hut. Or they could have buried him, in which case he might never have been found."

I frowned. " No, that won't do, because it would have made refrigeration and the time-factor superfluous."

Colonel Clay sighed in the gloom. " All right," he said, " let's not make it too complicated, shall we?"

He went nearer to the three constables and watched the operations from close range. I figured those fellows must have shifted about three tons of sand in the last couple of hours.

" Let's call it a night," he said at last. " I don't think we're going to be in luck."

The constables thankfully got to their feet and started packing up their equipment. Clay came over and joined me and Griffith, who was putting the last of his instruments back in his case. There was a strong smell of alcohol, heavy on the night air.

" I'll have another team look again in the morning," Colonel Clay said. " You never know, they might turn it up by daylight. Leave the flags," he added in a shout to the men behind him.

When we got up to the road again the patrol car which had taken Stella back to the Catamaran was in its old position. The radio was still spitting out instructions and static and the driver looked as bored as ever. I glanced at the luminous dial of my wrist-watch. It was already creeping on for half past three and I was beginning to feel the effects of delayed tiredness.

Griffith had his own car so we said goodnight.

" Report by nine o'clock," he told Clay. The police driver started his engine; I got in my own car with Colonel Clay

and the cortege started back down the twisting road in the
moonlight. The soft, broken mumble of the sea carried
clearly to us above the soft hum of the engine. We had to
go slowly because we were directly behind the ambulance.
The red crucifix stencilled on the rear door jolted and
gyrated on the bumpy road, as though pinned there by
the spotlight of our headlamps. It seemed a long way back
down to the hotel.

<h1 style="text-align:center">3</h1>

The Colonel had his headquarters at the small harbour
town of Stanley Bay, which served as the island's capital.
It was about seven miles farther on from the Catamaran,
so he stopped off at the hotel to complete his inquiries.
Looked like he was making a night of it.

"You don't mind?" he asked me apologetically. If this
had been in L.A. and the police had kept me up all night
I should have told him to go fry a stale yak egg, but he was
so polite and all that it never occurred to me.

"I'm on holiday," I told him.

The Colonel's eyes gleamed with suppressed amusement
but he only added mildly, "This won't take more than a
quarter of an hour."

We went on into the lounge of the hotel. Two or three
bored-looking waiters were standing around or hunched
in chairs at the side of the main hall. The manager was
nowhere about but McSwayne himself was standing behind the reception desk going through piles of paper with
a white police inspector. He didn't look too happy.

"Looks like you just lost a paying customer," I told
him. He grunted. The Inspector turned round then and
recognising the Colonel tore him off a smart salute, despite
the lateness of the hour. I was impressed.

"Oh," said the Colonel, fidgeting with his nose, "this

is Phillips. Mr. Faraday is helping us with the investigations."

The inspector was a pleasant-looking lad of about twenty-eight, I should have said. He gave me a rugged grin as we shook hands.

" Not much here, sir," he told Colonel Clay, leafing over the visitor's book.

I looked over his shoulder. Our friend out on the beach had registered himself as Carl Grosvenor with an address in North Chicago.

" We'd better have a look at his room," said Clay to McSwayne, " and then we'll call it a night." This last remark he addressed to me, with an apologetic sideways smile as he led the way up the staircase.

" You can let those fellows go to bed now," he said to Phillips. " We shall want them available for questioning tomorrow, of course."

I drew the Colonel to one side as Mr. McSwayne fumbled with the key in the lock of Grosvenor's room.

" I'll check on Grosvenor as well when I make that Chicago call tomorrow," I said. " If you can get a picture we can wire that for identification."

" There may be one in his room," said Clay.

" If not you'd better lay on a post-mortem picture tonight," I said.

The Colonel sucked in his cheeks for a second and then blew them out; I guessed what he was thinking without him saying anything. Death is pretty vulgar, I guess, though the English are good at smoothing it over.

However, all he said was, " We've got him on ice, so we should be able to get a fair likeness."

By this time McSwayne had got the door open and was looking impatient so we all trooped in. One coloured constable stayed outside the door, another constable and Clay turned the room up and the owner stood at the end of the bed looking like he'd just woken up in the middle of a nightmare. I went and sat down on the edge of the dressing-table and fought to keep awake.

If Clay thought he was going to hit the jackpot here he must have been mighty disappointed. Apart from the usual items of clothing; bathing trunks, toilet gear, beachwear, sandals and that sort of thing there was nothing personal at all. Even the valise Clay pounced on so eagerly yielded nothing of interest. I didn't know, of course, what Grosvenor's pockets contained: doubtless an inventory would be made at the morgue, or whatever they had on this island.

But, leaving that possibility aside for a moment, I'd never seen anyone travel with less to identify him than our lean friend. I thought again of his haunted, tired face as I had seen him in the corridor only half a day earlier, and I wondered what strange destiny had sent him out to meet his death at the hands of the two men I had seen in the boat. Unless he had been killed by someone else and the two men were merely carrying out a sombre form of delivery service. I hoped we would know in good time.

Even Grosvenor's spare clothing was bare of those small intimate objects that might have given us some inkling of his habits. I lit a cigarette and the thin rasp of the match over the box seemed to exasperate the nerves of Colonel Clay.

" All right," he snapped, turning to the constable. " That'll do for tonight, Mr. McSwayne. We'll have to seal this room. I'll leave one man on guard and we'll go over it again tomorrow."

" Don't forget the P.M. picture," I told Clay. He looked startled for a second or so.

" To wire to Chicago," I reminded him. He looked swiftly round the room and saw that the dressing-table was bare of photographs. He sighed. " Right," he said. We all went on out.

4

I leaned on the door of the patrol car and looked in through the wound-down window to where Colonel Clay sat drumming his fingers on the dash-cubby. The engine idled softly.

"There's just one thing," I asked him. "I don't carry any weapons on holiday and my Smith-Wesson's stashed away back in L.A. I'd feel more comfortable with a revolver of some sort. Things are apt to get rough on cases like this."

Colonel Clay turned his head towards me. "Sorry, Michael, that's right out of our style," he said. "Normally we don't carry firearms of any sort. Of course we have rifles and that sort of thing in case of riots or special emergency. But we have to get the go-ahead from Nassau. And unless it's something on the lines of an earthquake or tempest they won't play ball. I'm sorry, but there it is. And this isn't really on that scale, is it?" He smiled apologetically.

"All right," I told him. "We'll just have to wait and see how things go."

"Good man," he said. "If it's justified you can rely on me."

"I'm sure I can," I said.

"Well," he said wryly, looking at his wristlet-watch. "See you in a few hours' time. I'm going to get Nassau on the radio now and have a look at my reports. Let you know the situation in the morning."

He waved as the engine gunned and the car gathered speed as it moved off from the hotel forecourt. I went over to the hire Caddy, made sure I had locked it for the night and then went indoors.

Soon it would be dawn and I had a lot of sleep to make up. McSwayne had turned in but the manager and the

night porter were on duty. The manager looked as sore as
all hell. Inspector Phillips passed me on the stairs and said
a constable was on guard outside the late Grosvenor's door.

I looked at my watch; there didn't seem much point
in turning in after this, but I had to get some sack-time.
As I went up the corridor to my room, a door opened and
a figure in a dressing-gown ejected himself. He was fat, with
a red, mottled face, pig-like eyes and a greying mustache
lurking under his nose like it was ashamed to come out.
His breath smelt of drink and he looked mad. It was instant
distaste from the word go.

"Ha!" he said, waving a finger like a Frankfurter
sausage under my nose. "So you're one of these people
making all the noise around the corridors. It's getting so a
guest can't get to sleep. What the hell d'ye mean by it?"

I steered my way around him, but it didn't do any good.
He only caught hold of my arm and trundled alongside.
His breath was even worse than I expected.

"Go see the manager," I advised him.

"This is outrageous," he bleated. "You can't get away
with it like this. I shall take it up in the highest quarters."

"You do that," I said, giving him the broad of my hand
in his chest. It was only a gentle shove but he stumbled
back against the wall for just long enough for me to get
my key in the lock. He went puce.

"Thanks," I told him. "It was real nice." I closed the
door on his face; he looked like a fish fighting for breath.
It was only then that I saw the room wasn't in darkness.
There was a big shape sitting in the chair alongside my
bed. The barrel of the gun he held steadily aligned on my
navel looked like a Long Tom. It didn't waver any either.

"Make yourself at home," I said mechanically. His face
was hidden in the shadow cast by the bedside lamp but
I didn't have to hear his voice to place him. It was the big
muscle boy I had seen down at the Bonefish with my friend
in the red T-shirt.

" Don't make it rough for yourself, Mr. Faraday," the gorilla said. His voice sounded almost tired.

" I don't carry a gun on holiday," I said. He stood up then; his bulk seemed to block out all the light in the room.

" That's your story," he said.

" I couldn't break the Wolf Cub code," I told him.

He gave a sort of vulpine titter; he came over towards me. Close up, he seemed twice as big. I still couldn't see his face properly.

" I hope you're levelling—for your sake," he said. Just then there came a heavy bang at the door. The big fellow took two rapid hops towards the wall and the gun was back in his hand, rock-steady at my mid-riff.

" It's all right," I said. " I know who it is."

His gun barrel described two quick arcs in the air; he didn't say anything but the gesture was more eloquent than speech could have been. His eyes were quite expressionless. I opened the door a fraction. Alcohol fumes blew in my face. It was my fat friend with the skinful.

" I don't like your attitude," he sort of screamed at me. The Frankfurter was back under my nostrils again.

" I didn't know it showed," I said. That made him madder than ever.

" This is disgraceful," he spluttered. " I am a gentleman . . ."

" Come on over into the light," I said. " I always wanted to see what one looked like."

I felt something stir beside me and the big fellow was at my elbow. He eased round me to block the door. He was bigger still in the light from the hall. Judo or no judo I decided not to mix it with him unless I had to. He looked down at the little man almost amiably.

" Go pick your nose somewhere else, buster," he said gently. I couldn't see his face but it must have been pretty impressive, for the man in the dressing-gown just turned red. Then he spun on his heel and went.

The big fellow turned back to me; he put the gun back in his pocket and ran me over expertly with both hands.

"All right," he said, "get over in that chair and sit still. No funny stuff."

"Certainly," I said mildly. "It's been nice meeting you but do you mind if we take this up some other time? I've had a tiring day and I'd like to get to bed."

"This is just a warning," he said. "Don't mix it with us or you'll regret it."

"Thanks awfully," I said. "Sorry you had to come all the way out here just to tell me that. A postcard would have done just as well. Now, if you'd mind stating your business."

"You know what I'm talking about, shamus," he said. "Do I make myself clear? It ain't healthy . . ."

"Dear me," I said. "And I came out here specially for the purpose of improving my health. This hotel was specially recommended . . ."

"Just remember what I said," he grated, interrupting me. "Just to show you I ain't foolin' . . ."

He picked up a heavy wooden stool at the foot of the bed. Without exerting himself visibly he took it delicately in his two huge hands and plucked it apart, like I would the wings of a butterfly. There was nothing audible in the room but the splintering of wood; he sort of rolled the pieces of the stool between the palms of steel-hard hands and they almost fell to powder.

"I'll have to complain to the management," I said. "That stool must be full of woodworm."

The rest of the sentence was lost as he threw the remains down on the carpet with a restrained fury. He picked his gun from the end of the bed where he'd laid it, and it just melted back in his pocket.

"Remember, shamus," he repeated.

"Just tell the desk what you've done," I told him. "I don't want that put on my bill."

My door opened and then shut suddenly in the silence. I grinned and went over and locked it after him. I didn't think it was worth disturbing Colonel Clay. The big fellow was so strong we couldn't have detained him at the hotel. And he couldn't get off the island anyway.

I undressed quickly and got to bed. I was asleep almost as soon as my head touched the pillow. I was glad to see my nerves hadn't suffered.

CHAPTER FOUR

Cucumber Cool

I

I WAS awakened by the shrilling of the telephone at my bedside.

It was Stella.

" Do you know what time it is?" she asked. " Colonel Clay has already been on to Mr. McSwayne."

" Just a minute," I said. " I've got a mouth full of bedclothes and a throat like I've been sleeping out on the beach all night."

" I told you scampi doesn't agree with you," she said.

I cut her off short. She was beginning to sound like we were married. I looked at my watch. It was all of a quarter to eight.

" If he's coming out, tell him I'll meet him downstairs for breakfast at half-eight," I said. " I'll pick you up in about twenty minutes."

" I'll be in the shower," she said.

" I should be that lucky," I told her and rang off. I rolled over, looked up at the ceiling and wondered if my lower jaw was still connected to the upper half of my face. I sure felt rough. Late nights didn't agree with me like they used to. Still, it had been pretty late, even as late nights go.

I went over and looked at myself in the mirror. My face was a nice shade of lavender so I didn't stay long. I went into the bathroom and took a shower. Then I smoked as I dressed. I opened the big French doors leading on to the balcony and went out. The sea came creaming in from the Atlantic in long, lazy swells and met the dazzling pink and white sand down below the hotel. Sailboats were already dotted about and splashes and shrieks of girlish laughter came up from the big crescent-shaped pool in front of the terrace. They weren't all coming from girls either.

I smoked, took in the morning air and with it the perfume of the flowers and the wind off the sea. Then I thought of last night, the beach and the big ape with a neat line in chair-dismantling and a frown chased away my vision of the Garden of Eden. There were some dangerous snakes in the garden and we had agreed to smoke them out.

I finished dressing, put my room key in my pocket and went on out and down the corridor to Stella's room. A door shut somewhere as I passed but when I looked over my shoulder I couldn't place the sound and nothing was moving. Stella had a sailor-blue dress on to-day, very simple and child-like, except that it didn't look at all child-like on her. Not with that figure. She wore tiny jade earrings and she had some sort of bandeau arrangement holding back her hair; at any rate the general effect was good enough to alter my blood-rate, though I didn't let on to her.

As we went down to breakfast I filled her in on the latest developments. When I mentioned my visitor her eyes widened and she wrinkled her nose, though whether in distaste at my description of him or disgust at my not mixing it with his fifty stone, I had no way of knowing.

" He shouldn't be too difficult to trace," I said by way of excusing myself, " and he can't get off the island."

"Neither can you, chum," she said with a significant glance. I got her point.

"Cheer up," I said. "I'm sorry about the holiday but that's war."

She squeezed my arm. "Don't get too involved," she said. "Do you want me to come along and take notes?"

I shook my head. "No need for two of us. I couldn't very well help it the way the cards fell, and it seems to me Clay could do with some assistance. All these fellows carry is a glorified wooden walking stick."

She laughed. "Anyway, I hope we shall still see each other occasionally."

"It won't ruin the vacation," I said.

"I've heard that before," she told me. I couldn't top it so I didn't come back this time."

We went in to breakfast. McSwayne was looking a little more cheerful. He was sitting having his own breakfast with Mrs. McSwayne and two friends at the corner table permanently reserved for them. He came on over when he saw us sit down. On the way he passed a plump figure which was making its way furtively into the dining-room. As the two skirted each other, the red-faced one turned towards me and I recognised my fat friend of the night before. I gave him a hard stare.

He started, coughed and then went redder than ever. He pulled away pretty rapidly and set off at a heavy lope out through the dining-room and to an outside table. He made the water buffalo seem like an elegant beast. McSwayne sat down at my nod. He smoked moodily for a minute or two.

"Don't worry," I told him. "These things are just passing shadows."

He shrugged. "All the same, I wish I knew what Colonel Clay was up to. It gets a hotel like ours a very bad name."

"You're taking it to heart," I said. "He didn't die here, did he?"

He brightened. " No, that's true. And he could just as easily have been knocked down in a motor accident."

Then a frown chased across his face again. " All the same, I'd be glad to know when the Colonel plans to release the room."

" Why don't you ask him?" said Stella. " He's just coming in now."

The tall, grey-clad figure of the Colonel appeared on the terrace as she spoke. McSwayne looked relieved. " Guess I will," he said. He slid off the chair and stood up. " See you later."

The waiter came just then and we were ordering but when I looked up I could see the two of them standing on the terrace talking.

" Good morning, young lady. Good morning, Michael."

Clay, as he joined us, looked pleased with himself. He was relaxed, his hair and mustache were as trim as the morning, he was freshly shaved and bathed, and if I hadn't known better I'd have said he'd put in at least ten hours sleep the previous night.

He sat down almost jauntily and addressed himself to the oversize grapefruit the waiter immediately brought him.

" How did things go?" I asked him.

" Couldn't be better," he said. " Nassau were a bit dubious at first about our suggested arrangement, but they finally saw it my way."

By the faint smile I caught on his face, I gathered that it had been an amusing conversation. Stella said nothing and her face was buried in a cup of coffee, so I couldn't see her expression.

" Then we're in," I said.

" Precisely," said Clay, neatly spearing a segment of grapefruit with the sharp edge of his spoon. He lowered his voice. " I haven't exactly been idle after I left this morning."

" You could have fooled me," I said looking pointedly at his immaculately tailored figure.

" We got a rundown on the yachts at Stanley Bay last night, together with the general shipping movements," he said. " I've authorised the Chicago call and we can do that about midday. This is what I believe you wanted."

He passed over a closed pasteboard folder.

" Let me have the name of the officer concerned and the details and I'll put a copy of this on plane to Nassau so they can radio it to Chicago," he said.

I opened the little folder. It was rather like a passport, except that Carl Grosvenor looked rougher than when I had last seen him. Even so Doc Griffith had done a pretty good job on him. I've seen worse things in old Boris Karloff movies.

Griffith must have some trouble with the eyes, but he'd managed to get them open and the expression wasn't too bad; the police photographer had photographed him as though he were looking downward, and apart from a slight droop to the eyelids he looked pretty normal. But it was obvious Karsh hadn't taken it. I didn't show the picture to Stella. I didn't want to spoil her holiday.

" I'll hang on to this," I told Clay. " It might come in useful later."

Then I told him about my visitor. He looked at me narrowly and picked up his coffee cup. He didn't say anything for a minute. He just drained the cup and sat looking out over the sea. The only sign he gave was a light drumming of his fingers on the table top. Then he wiped his lips fastidiously with his napkin.

" I take it you've a very good reason for not calling me last night, Michael?" he said presently.

I finished off another piece of toast and reached for the marmalade again.

" It's like this, Colonel," I said. " Firstly, the guy was so big he could have taken the whole hotel apart. Secondly,

we didn't discuss anything, that could have tied him in with
a crooked roulette wheel, let alone a murder. Thirdly, he
can't get off the island. Fourthly, free, he may lead us to
someone else. And fifthly, it was a stupid deal to tip off his
hand like that. I figured if we kept him on the loose he
might lead us to better things."

The Colonel nodded. He was smiling now. "All right,
Michael," he said. "I'll go along with that. All the same
it may lead to considerable risk for you."

"That doesn't worry me," I said. "What I can't figure
is why he should have come right out in the open. Looks
like whoever he's working for is suffering from an overdose
of confidence. It was pretty cool stuff, what with the hotel
swarming with police and all."

"I take it you didn't discount that he might be a guest
at this hotel?" Stella asked quietly.

"Pretty good, sweetie," I said. "I had a word with
Inspector Phillips before we came in to breakfast. He's
checking the register and questioning the staff now. But
I don't think these boys are that stupid. Over-confident,
yes, but that would be pretty foolhardy."

I turned back to the Colonel. "Apart from risking a
charge of breaking into a guest's room Carnera didn't really
stick his neck out. He may have a licence for the gun, we
didn't discuss a thing of importance and he could have
told the hotel staff he'd gotten into the wrong room by
mistake. And it's only a hunch on my part that he and his
Chicago mobster chum were in that boat last night."

Stella got up as I finished speaking. "Well," she said,
"I expect you've got a busy day. I'll be on the beach if
you want me."

"See you for lunch," I said.

"Don't count on it," she said and went on out. I
watched her can until it was out of sight. Then I found
my cigarette butt was burning my fingers. Colonel Clay
was regarding me quizzically.

" What about those refrigeration plants?" I asked him defensively.

" We checked a couple at the main dock at Stanley Bay last night," he said. " A clean sheet as far as we can make out, but we've got to question all the labour force. They don't do any killing on the premises. I've got a list of another dozen places, three on adjoining islands."

He threw me over a sheet of typed paper. I saw it was headed, " Copy for Mr. Faraday "; I skimmed down the list of addresses. " Where do we go from here?" I asked him.

" Well," he said, " if you can spare the time, I thought we could run down to the office and get this photo-wire business sorted out. We've got the call itself fixed for midday. I'm having the mainland and the island ice depots checked but there's several on out islands. If I can get a spare launch we'll have a look at one or two places ourselves, time permitting."

" Suits me," I said. We went on out. I waved to the McSwaynes as we passed the window. The Colonel had his Alvis parked in the forecourt in front of the hotel. I sighed as I looked down towards the beach. A girl in a scarlet bikini was running into the surf, sending up sparkling diadems of spray that fell back into the sea like flecks of snow. It looked like Stella. I hoped we'd be back in time. I didn't know Stella had bought a bikini. This I had to see.

A shadow swept across the crowded swim-pool and the beat of a motor came to our ears. One of the inter-island planes that connected the island with Nassau sliced the blue, tilted its wings and settled up on course, heading out to sea. I sighed again and followed the Colonel out to the car.

2

The Colonel drove fast, but skilfully; usually I don't like being a passenger, but I felt safe with him. In no time at all, it seemed, we had arrived at Stanley Bay, and I felt the big hand which had been pressing my back into the up-holstery relax its grip, as he slackened speed. I caught the Colonel's eyes in the driving mirror; there was a slight spark of humour in them.

Stanley Bay was a bigger place than I had expected; we rolled down a broad boulevard between pink and white villas with open green lawns edged with scarlet and white flowers. A Union Jack floated listlessly from a flagpole and I caught a glimpse of a couple of old cannon looking out to sea over stone battlements.

A large yacht rode at anchor about a mile off shore, with a flock of sailboats moored around her. Then we turned a corner and were in the harbour proper. The Alvis made hardly any noise as we idled along a jetty, past cream painted warehouses and stores. The Harbour-Master's office slid by and the Colonel pulled the Alvis in to a space marked Police Vehicles Only. I followed him into a modest, two-storey stone building. It had trim manicured lawns around two sides of it and more cannon.

We went in a door under a sign painted black on white which said POLICE OFFICE : there was some kind of crest under it, but I didn't get time to see it. It was cooler inside; the office was painted pale-green and a native constable sat at a plain wooden table and fooled with a sheaf of papers. A fan circulated in the ceiling and through the big window facing the harbour I could see a couple of police launches dancing alongside a POLICE ONLY jetty.

Another constable was sitting near a small telephone switchboard and a native sergeant kept an eye on the whole show as he turned out reports on a neolithic typewriter. He gave Clay a broad smile as we went by. The Colonel led the way through a second door in back. His own office was painted cream and had a grey carpet. An identical view of the harbour was pasted outside the window.

There was a more ornate desk, three green telephones, an umbrella stand and Inspector Phillips riffing through the bumf in a regulation green filing cabinet which gaped open at the side of the room.

" Hullo, sir," he said as he caught sight of Clay. He nodded pleasantly at me. " I'm glad you came in. I'm just off down to North Shore Drive to check the deep freeze plant. Nothing you want me for in the meantime?"

" No thank you, Ian," Clay told him. " You've made out the report I take it?"

" On the desk, sir." Phillips nodded towards the window. " I'll take the truck then and get off. Nothing positive so far, I'm afraid. It's all in the report."

He nodded again and went on out.

" A good lad," Clay grunted, " but he's inclined to work too much on his own if I don't watch it. Too many forms though. I agree with him there."

He went and sat down at the desk and leafed through the mass of paper with an eloquent forefinger. Then he glanced up at me with apology. " Sorry, Michael. Take a pew, won't you?"

He indicated an armchair placed in front of the desk and I sat down. It was so comfortable I could have stayed there all day but I had other fish to fry. While he went through the report I studied the picture of Grosvenor again; he looked deader than ever. Then I wrote down the name of my friend in the Chicago Police and the details for the cable. When I had finished Clay got up and took the piece of paper outside. I heard him giving instructions to the sergeant. He came back in.

" We radioed Nassau earlier and they've laid everything
on," he said. " As soon as they hear from us now they'll
transmit the message and the picture to the Chicago police."

" The wonders of science," I said.

Clay went and stared thoughtfully out of the window at
the sea-sparkle and the yachts at anchor. " How long do
you think it will take?" he said.

" The Chicago call?" I told him. " Difficult to say. We
might get a reply by tomorrow if they have any record on
Grosvenor. But if the name and address are phoney it may
take quite a while. Of course the picture will simplify things
if he has a criminal record or his prints are on file."

Clay came back again and sat down at his desk and
shuffled his papers.

" Did you turn up anything in his room?" I asked.

He shook his head. " A complete blank. A negative too
on the ice depots, though we haven't finished there by any
means. These two fellows you saw must be on one of these
boats somewhere; we've had no reports from any hotels at
all and no-one like that has left from the airport. The only
plane out in the last twenty-four hours carried fourteen
passengers and half of those were women and children."

He sighed and reached for his cigarettes. I noticed he had
a silver cigarette box on the desk. I took one of the Russians
with the cardboard cylinder, from the other side of the box.
There's no sense in carrying anti-Communism too far. It
was a good cigarette.

" I wish I had a bigger staff," said Clay. " What we really
need is a boat-to-boat search, but that may take days."

" Cheer up," I said. " This guy is too big to hide in-
definitely. Do you mind if I take a look at the yacht register, or whatever it is you've got there?"

He passed over a sheaf of paper. I soon saw there must
have been something like two hundred boat names on it.
He saw the look on my face and chuckled.

" This covers every harbour and bay on the island," he

said. " I don't propose to search every duck-punt, if that's
what you were thinking. We've marked every sizeable craft
with an asterisk and we've eliminated those owned by
residents known to us."

I thumbed down the list. The biggest boat there was
The Gay Lady. I looked out of the window again.

" That the one?" I asked.

He nodded. " We haven't been aboard yet. Belongs to a
millionaire fellow from New York, according to our
records."

I went over to the hat-stand and opened up a brown
leather case that was hanging there.

" Do you mind?" I asked. I put the glasses to my eyes.
They were made by Zeiss, of course, as I had guessed they
would be and the magnification of the coated lenses brought
up the detail of *The Gay Lady* in startling close-up. I looked
out at the yacht for a quarter of an hour. I don't know what
I was looking for, but if it was a big man with a little
fellow I was sure disappointed.

There was a big, chunky man though; he wore white
drill trousers and a white, open-neck shirt. From the way the
crew behaved when they passed around him, I took him
to be the owner. I couldn't see his face properly; it was too
far, even for these glasses. He stood under an awning in the
stern of the yacht and smoked a cigar. I could see the thick
blue smoke clearly in the sunshine. He didn't move all the
time I watched him. I put down the glasses thoughtfully.
The Colonel sat watching me.

" What about this ice depot you were talking about?" I
said.

" You've got the list in your pocket," he said. " I thought
the Ajax Company might be a good place for us to start.
It's on one of the nearer islands."

I had another look at the list. The Ajax Cold Storage
Company was at a place called Cucumber Cay. That didn't
tell me much.

"You'd better have this," added the Colonel, throwing me a letter. "You'll find it more useful than a gun out here."

It was a brief document on police notepaper to say that the bearer, one Michael Faraday, had the sanction of the island police force and was to be afforded every facility by members of the general public, etc., etc. It was signed by Colonel Clay at his most official and had some sort of imposing stamp at the bottom of it.

"Thanks," I said and put it in my wallet. By this time it was nearly half-eleven and we would be putting through the call at midday. It had to go through Nassau which was the reason for all the palaver. I could see Clay had some more paperwork to attend to so I excused myself and strolled down to the jetty. I had a look at the two police launches; they were powerful jobs and I was interested to see they were fully equipped, with searchlights. I looked through the wheelhouse windows of one and could see a crowded carbine rack fixed into the bulkhead. So much for Colonel Clay's unarmed police force, I thought, but I guess there is some difference between revolvers carried on the person and rifles. And they might well need the latter at sea. I stared out across towards *The Gay Lady* again but the figure in the stern had gone. It was now around ten to twelve so I strolled back to the office. After a few minutes the switchboard constable called Clay over; he handed the mouthpiece to me. There was a lot of static on the line but the voice was surprisingly clear. "Barney?" I said. It had been a person to person call but I couldn't recognise his tones at first.

Barney had been quite a chum of mine when he worked with the official force in L.A. under Captain Dan Tucker about half a dozen years before. Now he was a Captain of Detectives in Chicago and if anyone could find out anything about Grosvenor he was the guy best equipped to do it.

We chit-chatted for a minute or so and then I got down

to business; it was an expensive call and I knew Clay had his eye on the office clock. I thought he was afraid the Queen would give him a hot-foot if he couldn't justify his expenses sheet at the end of every month.

I told Barney the set-up and he confirmed that the photograph had been radioed and was going through Records at that moment. There was something else fretting around the back of my mind; I hadn't mentioned it to the Colonel because it was so nebulous but it strengthened the Chicago angle.

" I ran into a little man down here who might know something about it, but I can't place him," I said. " I saw him in a police line-up in L.A. about two years ago and his face stayed in my mind. He's a little guy with mean eyes. Sorry I can't be more specific. I think he was booked in L.A. for suspected armed robbery if that helps any. But I know he worked out of Chicago and had a police record there."

Barney took the details down. I looked at Clay. His face was expressionless but the constable was smiling. Barney said he'd come back on the wire at the same time tomorrow. I thanked him and hung up.

" Thank you, Michael," said Clay, leading the way out of the office. One of the constables followed us, walking a couple of yards behind. We went down to the jetty.

" You didn't mention anything about this other man," Clay said as we walked.

" It's all very vague," I said. " It's the same little man who was in the boat with the big fellow. I didn't want to say anything until I had something better to go on."

He nodded. " Well, thanks again. You've already been a tremendous help. This might not be so difficult as we think."

He seemed remarkably optimistic, I thought, but I kept it to myself.

3

" If you don't mind, Colonel," I said, " I'd like to spend a quarter of an hour on the jetty before we shove off."

He hesitated. " Why, surely, if you really want to . . ."

" I've got a good reason," I told him.

He had his glasses dangling from a leather strap slung over his shoulder. I tapped the case with my finger.

" If you can make yourself inconspicuous in the launch," I said, " keep your glasses trained on *The Gay Lady* for the next quarter of an hour. You may see nothing, but on the other hand it might be interesting."

He got down into the launch, sat on one of the stern lockers and started focussing the binoculars. I went down the jetty a way. I knew what I was looking for. Every seaport however small always has one of them. There's always a longshore loafer who knows all the news of the harbour, who sits all day in the sun and runs the occasional errand for the price of a drink.

Sure enough, it didn't take me long to find him. He was a thin, melancholy-looking man with dim, watery eyes and a peaked nose. His comic-opera-type striped jersey only accentuated his thinness and his ancient, gold-leafed yachting cap was liberally spotted with bird-droppings.

" He stoppeth one in three," I said to myself.

" Eigh," he mumbled, looking at me apprehensively. He obviously hadn't heard of Coleridge, and it wouldn't have done any good if I'd told him, so I let the point slide.

" I'm looking for some information, dad," I told him.

" Well, I don't know about that," he said. We shook hands and as his palm came into contact with the rustling paper another expression came into his eyes. He looked down at the note which sort of quickly undulated its way into the pocket of his faded blue pants.

" That's different," he said. " Anything to 'blige a stranger."

He was an American for sure, but I couldn't place his accent. I took out the photograph of Grosvenor. The death hadn't yet been released to the Press and in any case the news had been too late for today's edition, so it was quite safe.

" Have you seen this man around lately?"

He took the piece of paper and squinted at it, shielding his eyes against the sun.

" What's he done? Welshed on his washing machine payments?" he said with a snickering laugh.

" He's an old friend of mine," I said. " I was told he was staying on the island and I'm trying to trace him."

He looked at the picture again. I was pretty sure he'd seen him before he spoke.

" Looks like some other friends got to him first," he said with another whinnying laugh. I looked at him sharply.

" Meaning what?" I said.

" Saw him just yesterday," he replied. " Think he's staying up at Catamaran on t'other side of the island. He went fishing in the afternoon with two guys. They hired a boat just down the jetty there."

He jerked a tobacco-stained finger in the direction of a Boat Hire sign farther down the boardwalk.

" Didn't seem very keen on goin', though. They was almost draggin' him last I saw of of 'em."

I looked at him again. " A big guy and a little fellow?" I asked.

He met my gaze unwaveringly. " That's right. They friends of yours?"

" I think I know them," I said. " You didn't think this was peculiar?"

" Weren't no business of mine," he said almost defiantly. " Listen, son, I been setting on this jetty takin' the sun for the last thirty years and I seen some pretty peculiar characters come and go. Don't pay to be too nosey. I aim to go on restin' my ass for the next thirty, God willin'.''

" Yeah, well make sure your big end doesn't give out," I told him. " Thanks for the information."

He spat and settled himself more comfortably on the low stone wall he was using as a seat. I paused before turning away.

" You didn't happen to hear where they were going?" I asked.

He shook his head. " Too far away."

I left him and went back towards the pier and the police launches. As I came up Clay turned towards me. He handed me the glasses.

" Boat going out now," he said.

I focussed up just in time to see a dinghy driven by a small outboard pass round the counter of *The Gay Lady*. I couldn't make out the seaman in the brief glimpse but I could see the small runt in the red T-shirt sitting in the stern, except that now he was wearing a jersey with *Gay Lady* in white letters stitched across it. I handed the glasses back to the Colonel.

" That's the man," I said. " But I'd let things lie for a bit if I were you. We've got nothing but suspicions to go on for the moment. Best to keep an eye on who comes and goes from the yacht and bide our time."

" Sensible advice," said Clay. " Did you learn anything?"

He looked back down the jetty and I realised he had seen my talk with Sinbad.

" Jackpot," I said. I told him what I had found out. He looked pleased.

" You get aboard and make yourself comfortable," he said. " I'll have a watch put on the yacht. One of the chaps can easily do this from the office window without anyone being the wiser. And I must get some information out. I won't be five minutes."

He went back up along the jetty and disappeared. Five

minutes passed, then ten. I got fidgety and went back up
the path. When I got near the police officer I met Clay
coming back down. At the same time my friend with the
broad behind came round one of the ornamental cannon.

"I just remembered somethin'," he called out, as he
met us at the corner of the path.

"I'm sorry, Michael," Clay said with a gesture of disgust.
"I've got bogged down. Phillips wants me to come over
and sort something out on North Shore Drive. Senior officer
and all that."

He smiled wryly. "Unless you'd like to run over to
Cucumber Cay with the constable. It would be a big
help . . ."

The rest of his words were drowned as the dock-side
loafer caught hold of my arm. "That's it," he screeched
triumphantly. "That's the place. I remember now. That's
where the three fellows were going fishing yesterday."

I stared at him. Things were beginning to add up fast.

"Where's Cucumber Cay?" I asked automatically, for-
getting that Clay and the constable would know.

Sinbad clutched at my arm again. "It's Cucumber Cay,"
he said. "It's called that on account it's a cucumber shape."

"I thought it was triangular," I said. He blinked but
said nothing.

"Well, yes," said Colonel Clay clearing his throat
awkwardly.

"Now let's consider these points, Michael."

We started walking back to the jetty. "The Cay is about
four miles down," he said. "Just a short trip. It may mean
missing lunch, of course, but it'll be another useful check."

"Pleased to do it," I said.

I jumped on board the launch. The constable was
already casting off. He saluted as Clay gave him his instructions. The engine was opening up to a muffled roar
and Clay's hurrying figure was already minute. I saw that
the loafer had already gone back to his seat on the wall.

I hadn't thanked him but no matter. He had my gratitude in his pocket, where it would do him most good.

As we made the harbour entrance—it was really two overlapping stone moles—we passed within a few hundred yards of *The Gay Lady*. She was a pretty impressive lay-out and sparkled with brass and white paintwork. I got down off my conspicuous position leaning on the cabin top and sat in the stern just in case anyone was looking over but nothing moved.

It was already a quarter to one and like the Colonel said looked like I should miss my lunch. As soon as we cleared the harbour the constable opened her out and we started to cream through the water, throwing up spray in a slight ground swell that had started. He kept about a mile off shore and after about a quarter of an hour I could see a long, low shape coming up to starboard.

" Cucumber Cay," said the constable, spinning the wheel professionally to bring the nose of the big launch round. I offered him a cigarette and as we smoked he enlarged on our destination.

" Nothin' there but the refrigeration plant. They got a jetty on the seaward side. They kill cattle on the spot as well as store meat and they're able to load and unload cargo in deep water."

I soon saw what he meant. We were doing about twelve knots and as the constable started his run in to the landward side of Cucumber Cay, I could see the jetty he had spoken of, jutting out, a black, fretted shape against the sea-silver on the ocean side.

He idled in to a small pier and tied up. White sand ran inshore to meet shrubby vegetation and limestone. The place didn't exactly look a hive of industry. Half a dozen concrete buildings were visible through the trees, there were pens and outbuildings, and I could hear the deep-chested lowing of cattle somewhere above the mumble of the surf.

" Stay here," I told the constable. He looked surprised and disappointed.

" It's only a routine check," I told him, " but in case of trouble you could do far more good by getting word back to Colonel Clay. Keep your eyes peeled and if I'm not back inside an hour sound the siren. If that doesn't raise me within a few minutes get off-shore and back to Stanley Bay."

He nodded and waved as I jumped off the boat and on to the boards of the rickety jetty. I walked away inland, until I came on a dusty path through the stunted vegetation. A big black and white sign, faded with years of exposure to the harsh sun, spelled out; AJAX COLD STORAGE COMPANY : PRIVATE. I went on in through a gap between the buildings. There didn't seem to be anyone around. The back of the place was filled with old oil drums and other gear.

It was bigger than I had thought. The humming of generators filled the air and I passed several open-sided lairage pens filled with cattle and sheep which gave off a warm stench, strong and unmistakable from under the big tin roof which protected them from the sun.

I came round a corner a bit sharply and almost ran into a coloured labourer coming up from the jetty I could now see on the other side. He looked startled but he didn't change his expression when I showed him my typed sheet from Colonel Clay.

" That's all right, sah," he said, handing it back to me incuriously. " Look around all you want. Mr. Frost's gone over to Stanley Bay this afternoon but I guess he won't mind. He'll be back in around an hour if you got the time to spare."

I thanked him and went on across a cleared space towards a long row of concrete deep freeze chambers; these were what I was mainly interested in. They were under a big overhanging steel roof with a concrete apron and loading bay underneath. A row of electric trucks stood off on one side, evidently used for transporting sides of beef.

The whine of electrical machinery filled the air and there was a big switchboard labelled; DANGER in red letters a foot high. Then I saw why the place was so open. Vast sliding wooden doors were folded back and there was a metal groove in the floor so that the whole place could be closed up. I guessed it made operations easier when they were unloading a whole cargo into the chambers at the same time.

I picked number six, the farthest freezer on the right-hand side. It looked the oldest of the bank, but apart from that nothing distinguished it from the others. The door was painted red and it had big black metal hinges. On the outside were locks and temperature gauges, but the whole thing at the moment was merely closed by the heavy steel latch. I lifted this and found myself sweating as I pulled the big door back. That didn't last for long.

A blast of Arctic air hit me. I saw the lamps inside shining on thousands of ice crystals, the muslin-sheeted shapes of the carcasses on rails reaching in to the far distance. Lights burned evenly down the centre of the ceiling and my breath came frostily out of my throat.

I knew I had to be quick if I wanted to work through these sheds without freezing up; I stepped inside and found it necessary to button my coat right up to the collar straight away. I saw a slaughter-man's heavy overall knee-length coat hanging up on a rack outside the freeze-chamber and put that on over the top.

I just wanted to make sure of something else before I went inside. By its design I felt sure this chamber had been built long before the war; modern set-ups cut off the interior lighting as soon as the outer door is closed. I stood just inside the entrance and then pulled the door shut. It closed with a click but the lights stayed on. This was useful; I had a small pocket fountain-pen torch on me, but this was a place I wouldn't want to get lost in the dark.

There was a big lever just inside the door. I pulled this

C

over and heard the latch on the outside click into the off position. I pushed the door wide about six inches and jammed a meat cleaver in the bottom to keep it open. Then I saw a rack near the chamber and went outside again. There was a collection of compressed air pistols for killing cattle. They were used for shooting a steel bolt into the animal's brain. I don't know why, but I picked up a couple of these and carried them into the freezer with me.

My breath came up like steam and my footsteps echoed hollow as I went down between the rows of frozen carcasses. I was walking on ice, almost breathing ice. I took a look at the thermometer just beyond the second bay; it was way down, and I didn't scratch the frost away from the base to see just how far. What I could see was cold enough.

There was rack after rack of mutton and beef carcasses and it soon became obvious that I was unlikely to find much here; what was I looking for, I asked myself. Bloodstains? A button? Some frail hint that Grosvenor had been literally butchered in a scientific manner, with a row of sheep's heads looking on? I had to grin to myself. It was a pretty macabre idea and I felt like a walking corpse myself as I made the rounds.

There was only one way in and presently I came up against a steel end-wall, and retraced my way back along the second aisle of the compartments. There were racks at each side wall and then two more in the middle, dividing the chamber into two. There was no other sound but the soft hum of generators and the place felt remote from the world.

I picked up the two pistols from the bench where I had laid them and carried them out with me. I say out, but that was a pretty optimistic word under the circumstances. When I got to the entrance I saw that someone had been there before me. The meat cleaver had gone from the position I had left it, and the door was closed. I gave an experimental pull on the lever but, as I had expected, it gave an inch or two and then I heard the click of the big latch outside as it came up against the locking bolt securing it.

I would have sweated if it hadn't been so cold.

"Thanks for leaving the light, you bastard," I said to no-one in particular. I lit a cigarette and the little flame made a pleasing sight. I put back the two pistols on the floor and sat down on a bench to think things out and have a smoke.

CHAPTER FIVE

The Ice-Man Cometh

I

I DIDN'T sit there long. The cold was bone-penetrating. I glanced at my watch. Though the position was serious it wasn't dangerous and I wasn't perturbed. The aptly-named Mr. Frost should soon be back, one of the workmen could open up the deep-freeze chamber, the constable would report back to Clay, anything could happen. As a gambit by our opponents it was indecisive. But it was damned uncomfortable, I had to admit.

The only part I couldn't really understand was the light left burning—unless it had been to entice me in. Modern plants usually worked on the opposite principle, the light switching off as soon as the door was closed. Lucky for me though. I smiled at that, though it nearly cracked my lip. Some luck Faraday; right now I should have been tucking into the Catamaran's lunch special in a temperature way up in the top eighties. Still, they couldn't say a P.I. didn't get variety.

I stood up and flexed my arms and then stamped about for a bit. That was great. It made me realise just how cold it was. My watch glass already had a thin casing of ice over it; I couldn't see the temperature on the big wall thermometer—not that I wanted to see it anyway. I picked up one of the pistols and winced as my hand came into contact with it. I wrapped my handkerchief round the barrel and crashed it against the big main door of the vault.

It made a boom like all the clappers of hell, but for all the effect it had on my situation I might just as well have been an ant trying to punch its way out of a two-inch thick felt bag. I tried another half dozen blows but the only result was to crack long strips of ice off the main door; it seemed to be made of sheet steel. I started walking the whole length of the deep freeze—that way I might get some ideas and at least it would help to keep me warm. The cold was already penetrating my clothing; I began to calculate to myself how soon it would take me to freeze. It might not be so long as I had figured.

And of course, if anyone didn't come within the next few hours then things would be serious. I looked at my watch again. I had already been imprisoned just over an hour; though it wouldn't have given time for Clay to have received a message yet. Assuming the constable had obeyed my instructions, he would have waited at least an hour before sounding off with his siren. That would have been about now—though I certainly wouldn't have heard it penned up here. Any minute he would be setting off back to Stanley Bay—providing he hadn't been prevented from doing so. That was another point I didn't like thinking about.

There were so many imponderables that I gave up and devoted all my attention to the freeze chamber. I totted up assets; not very much under the circumstances, unless you counted the two pistols for humane-killing, my fountain pen flash and the miscellaneous contents of my pockets. The humming of the generators of the freeze-unit set my thoughts turning in the direction of the current supply, but as I expected there were no interior cables or switch gear and any trunking or conduit there might be was thickly iced over and would not be easy to locate.

I could see that it wasn't going to be a very amusing afternoon. And I couldn't do anything clever with the light fitting, even if I'd been that handy with electricity, because I should then be left in the dark. I tried the door lever again when my pacing next brought me opposite but it remained immovable. I gave the door another pounding but all that did was to loosen some more splinters of ice. I listened again but there was nothing but the whine of the generators. I thought of the shimmering heat only a few yards away from the door and knew what a turkey must feel like when it gets to Christmas Eve.

I gave the deep-freeze another once-over, before lighting my second cigarette. I had some idea that the generating plant was situated over the top of freezer chambers, obviously for technical reasons and this place was no exception. The humming of the generator sets was loudest at a point almost where I was standing, inside the big main door. I tested this by walking to and fro, but it always brought me back to the same spot, give or take a foot or two. Over the roof where I figured the generators might be was solid ice, the same as the rest of the walls, but there might be an inspection trap or some sort of panel for maintenance purposes underneath those crystals.

Apart from relying on luck, this was the only alternative I had; it didn't take me long to make up my mind. I hadn't stayed in business by pushing my chances where luck was concerned and right now I needed the exercise for warmth. Using the skirt of my long coat for a glove I dragged a half-empty meat rack over to a point I judged the most promising. The more modern freezing plants had a sort of room over the chamber where all the maintenance work could be done; but this was an old job and they might have designed it with an unlocking panel to get at the machinery, whenever they de-frosted the freezer. Anyway, it was worth a try.

I piled up a half a dozen carcasses on the rack as a platform and found I could sit in reasonable comfort on top in order to scrape away at the ceiling; the humming was much louder here and I could feel the vibration through the metal plating the ice covered. One of the steel hooks on the rack served me as a useful tool; I bound my pocket handkerchief round it for a handle and started scraping away. The ice was old, tough and very, very cold; it seemed to breathe out a freezing vapour over my face and the splinters as I worked pricked my cheeks and tinkled down to the floor among the racks and sides of meat.

I didn't seem to be making much progress but at least it was better than sitting around waiting to ice over and after a few minutes I began to feel a little warmer. I looked at my watch again; I was surprised to see that it was more than two hours since I was locked in. By now I had enlarged an area about as big as a small handkerchief. I put my face up against the ceiling and started to examine the surface.

I was looking for small irregularities in the ice. They would be screw holes or slots in the inspection plate. After a short while I found a disc of caked ice. I raked it over with the hook; some of the surface chipped away, but the bump didn't disappear. I put my face up against it and breathed. I repeated this three or four times and when I put the hook at it again I saw a circular shape beneath the last thin coating of ice.

What I was looking at was the head of a screw; it was a big flat thing about as big as a dollar and it had a large slot across it. I frowned. It looked like one of those gimmicks that need a special tool to undo it. And that was just what I hadn't got. However, I kept making with the meat hook and breathing on the ice at intervals and eventually I got right down to the metal.

I could see a small crack opening up which I took to be the edge of the panel. This was encouraging. I fished in my pocket with half-frozen hands; there was a choice between coins and a pen-knife. I decided to save the knife for emergency and try the coins first. The experiment was encouraging. After some fiddling about I was able to get the coin to fit the slot but I couldn't shift it; after I had breathed on it a few times something gave, and the screw started to turn, slowly at first and then faster. It fell clittering to the floor and when I pulled at the edge of the plate a sheet of ice came away; I felt a tiny current of warm air and the noise of the generator was louder. I didn't exactly cheer but it wasn't a bad feeling. Half an hour later I had shifted three more screws and uncovered the whole side of an inspection panel about two feet long; I put my half-frozen hands into the slit between the roof and the edge of the plate and levered myself off the meat rack.

There was a grating shriek as I fell to the floor and the plate tore back. I landed on my feet, slipped and prevented myself from falling by catching hold of a metal upright. I was panting heavily. I glanced up at the roof; the plate hadn't come right away but it had bent back all along its length. I could see machinery inside and now and again a blue spark from a dynamo brush; I picked up the first of the stunning pistols and prayed that it hadn't frozen sufficiently to prevent it from operating properly.

I climbed stiffly back up on top of the rack and balanced myself on the meat carcasses. I carefully sighted the barrel of the pistol to put the bolt where it would do most good; it just fitted against one of the air vents in the end of the dynamo motor. My hand and the pistol were inside the inspection chamber; I levered my body to one side, behind the shield of the bent plate, braced myself as best I could and squeezed the trigger. The pistol jerked in my hand as the compressed air went out with a whoosh, there was a bang and the metal bolt spanged back across the deep freeze chamber with infinite force, splintering frozen particles of ice about the area in a white fringe. The whine of the dynamo went on.

I looked back inside the machinery room. The bolt had made a deep scratch in the edge of the metal of the air vent, instead of going on through. I only had one more pistol and one more bolt, so I had to get it right this time. I soon saw that I hadn't allowed for the heavy rim of the pistol barrel, which had sent the bolt into the metal instead of on through. I tested the distance with the second pistol and tried again.

This time I got it right. It was pretty spectacular under the circumstances. The pistol hissed again, the bolt spat through the dynamo vent and a fraction later there was an explosion followed by a sheet of flame; pieces of metal flew about the room, there were clouds of acrid smoke, the smell of burning rubber and the machinery stopped. I jumped down off the rack again. The lights flickered for a moment and then steadied. There was a heavy silence. I took a turn about and lit another cigarette. Now all I could do was wait.

2

" I'm real sorry about this, Mr. Faraday," said Mr. Frost for the fourteenth time. A tall, balding man in his forties, with horn-rimmed glasses, he blinked nervously around at the debris in the freeze chamber. A native sergeant with an overcoat round his shoulders fumbled at a meat-rack; a glum-faced white photographer took pictures as though he had no conviction they would come out, and if they did that they would be of any use.

It was now about six in the evening and I felt I had had enough. I had been outside to de-ice myself for the last half-hour and had just come back in to collect Clay. He

looked grim-faced as he conferred with Frost. He had
been away on the other side of the island when the constable
got back with the launch; hence the delay. It could have
been serious but fortunately the manager had let me out
before Clay and a launch-load of police turned up.

He had been checking on the chambers and had found
a one-degree drop in temperature on the dial outside. I
thought I'd never forget his face when he'd opened the door.
It would have been comic except to me it was the most
welcome sight in the world right then. But after the shock
he seemed more worried about the damage to the refrigeration chamber than anything else.

" No sign of Henaway?" Clay asked him. Henaway was
the Bahamian handyman I had bumped into on my arrival
at the island. Frost shook his head.

Clay turned a worried face towards me. " In with the
others, obviously," he said.

" Probably locked me in himself," I said.

Clay turned back to Frost. " We'll search the Cay before
my men leave," he said. " If you hear anything let us know
pretty sharp."

Frost nodded.

" Your people had better give this place a thorough
going-over," I said. " Ten to one this was where Grosvenor
got it. Though I doubt if we'll ever find anything useful."

Clay went back into the chamber and gave some instructions to the native sergeant. I went on out; the air was a
warm temperature and the sea, pale green and indigo was
slapping lazily at the rocky shore. I went and took some
deep breaths and stared at the sea and the sky and the real
estate. There were footsteps behind me and I turned to find
Clay, the police launch coxwain and Frost.

" Sorry about your freezer," I told the latter mechanically. " No hard feelings," he smiled. We shook hands and
then Clay and me and the constable walked back down to
the water's edge and got into the launch. I sat down in a

seat in the stern and smoked as the constable fooled with the wheel and jockeyed the launch out from the shore. Then and only then he started up the engine. I began to realise I was hungry. I looked up to see Clay's eye on me; he still looked worried.

"Relax," I said. "It wasn't your fault. I shouldn't have gone in alone. And anyways, there's no harm done."

He stiffened his jaw. "All the same, Michael," he said, "it's about time we had a showdown with those people on the yacht."

I shook my head. "Play it my way," I advised him. "As it is we haven't got a thing on them. Leave them alone for a day or two and they'll give themselves away."

He looked gloomy as he gazed out over the water that chopped past the swiftly-moving launch.

"Just as you say, Michael," he said, "but I hope you know what you're doing."

"A little patience won't hurt," I advised him. "That's just what our friends haven't got. I'm the only one they're gunning for at the moment. They won't do anything drastic until they're sure I know too much. This is their way of warning me off. Crude, but effective with some people."

"I hope you're right," he said, echoing his former words. "I've go to do some explaining in Nassau if anything happens to you."

I looked at him sharply but I couldn't make out whether he was serious or having a little joke.

"I know I'm right," I assured him, feathering out smoke through my nostrils. The tobacco tasted cool and fresh on an empty stomach. Despite the softness of the air I could still feel ice in my bones.

The Colonel was silent. Then he spoke again.

"Let's hope so, Michael, let's hope so," he said.

I sat and watched the friendly outlines of Stanley Bay coming up the far horizon.

3

I finished my second brandy and sat in my chair. It wasn't perhaps the most satisfying moment of my life but it ran it pretty close. In the background the samba band vibrated, round us was the murmur of voices of bored, contented people and on the table lay the remains of a dinner that wasn't exactly unpalatable, even by the Catamaran's high standards.

" So what did you do then?" said Stella. Her face, glowing with sun and the effect of the wine smiled impishly.

" Like the Titanic passenger ' Steward, I ordered ice, but this is ridiculous '," I said.

Even Colonel Clay joined in the laugh.

" Nevertheless, this is a bad business, Michael," he said. " Can't you get him to take things seriously, young lady?" he added, turning to Stella.

She puckered up her face. " I've known him for nearly four years now, Colonel, and he's never been any different," she said.

" Let's change the subject," I said. " We shall know more tomorrow when we get that call from Chicago. In the meantime there's no sense in wasting the evening."

The Colonel smiled agreement. After we finished he got up from the table and went out on the dance floor with Stella. I sat and smoked and watched them. He danced pretty well for an old guy I thought. Though he was straight, with shoulders hard back, he knew how to relax; his footwork was pretty nifty too. Evidently Stella thought so also; last time I saw her she had her head on his shoulder. I thought the Colonel looked red and uncomfortable as he danced past me. That made me smile again.

Around eleven we broke up; we walked the Colonel down to his car. He was driving the Alvis on this occasion.

The moon-shimmer danced on the polish and chrome of the bonnet as he sat in the driveway of the Catamaran with the engine idling almost inaudibly.

" Come to breakfast," I said. " Around nine a.m.?"

" This is getting to be a habit," he said. But he didn't sound displeased. Then I saw that he was looking at Stella. She chuckled quietly in the gloom beside me.

" All right," he said. " Then we'll go down to the office later and take that call."

He waved once and then went quietly out of the entrance and whispered along the lane. I heard the crackle of the exhaust a short while after that, but not until he got about a quarter of a mile away. There were plenty of people sleeping round about and the Colonel was always a considerate man.

I went back inside with Stella, said goodnight to McSwayne and we went up to our rooms. We stood on the balcony for a moment before going our ways; the little fountain tinkled in the forecourt and I thought of Grosvenor once again. Not as I'd last seen him on the beach but the queer, strained look he'd given me as he went past that afternoon—almost like he'd known he hadn't got long to go.

As though she knew what I was thinking. Stella tightened her fingers on mine.

" You'll be careful, Mike, won't you?" she whispered. I nodded. She kissed me very lightly on the mouth and then slipped away. I heard her door close very softly. I smoked one final cigarette before going in. I gum-shoed my way silently along the corridor, walking on the balls of my feet like I did in L.A. when I was on a job. I don't know why, except maybe because of an inborn caution after last night. I stopped as I got near to my door. There was a thin bar of light coming from underneath and spilling on to the carpeting of the hall.

I knew I hadn't left any lights on when I came down

earlier and the chambermaids didn't go to guests' rooms in the evening. I tip-toed very quietly over to the door and tried it. It was unlocked. I eased back the handle, pushed it open quickly and stepped aside. I looked round the lintel cautiously; the room seemed to be empty but there was a curious atmosphere that I couldn't place at once.

I walked in and shut the door behind me. Then I caught it again, the subtle aroma of a woman's perfume. I went on over near the bed and stopped. There was the scrape of a match followed by a flame as someone lit a cigarette. Then I saw that the bed wasn't empty.

There was a beautiful bare pair of shoulders on the pillow. Above was a mass of golden hair spread out over the bed. It was the sports job in the polka-dot bikini. She gave a low chuckle.

" Come on in," she said.

CHAPTER SIX

Mafia

I

" I'm GOING to get this door-lock changed," I said. " This place is about as private as Stanley Bay Bus Station."

She chuckled. She drew at her cigarette, blew out the smoke and patted the coverlet. " Come and sit down," she said.

" Thanks," I said. I was beginning to wonder if it was my room. I looked round. She seemed to guess my intention and threw me her packet. I took a cigarette out of the blue and gold package. She leaned forward and lit it with a slim gold lighter. I drew in the smoke.

The night wind came in at the big balcony windows, bearing with it the scent of many flowers; the noise of the sea was faint but clear while nearer at hand the slap of water still sounded where a solitary swimmer got in the last dip of the day at the marble pool at the edge of the hotel grounds.

" What are you doing here?" I said. " Or shouldn't I ask?"

She shrugged as she drew on her cigarette. I went and sat down in a chair at the side of the bed. I dragged it over where I could watch her face in the pale slice of light cast by the bedside lamp.

" Worried?" she said.

" Anxious about my reputation," I said. She laughed then.

" I suppose I should introduce myself. Diane Morris."

" My name's Faraday."

" I know," she said.

" That still doesn't explain what you're doing in my bed," I told her.

" I wanted to talk to you," she said. I said nothing but smoked on and waited. She drew on the cigarette and frowned to herself. The frown looked good on her.

" How did you get in?" I said.

" Not very difficult," she said. " I told one of the maids I'd forgotten my key. She didn't know it wasn't my room."

" Like my visitor last night," I said. " You wouldn't know anything about that?"

" I might," she said.

" Genial fellow," I said. " Goes in for breaking furniture with his bare hands."

She smiled. " That would be Otto."

" Friend of yours?" I asked.

She shook her head. " Not so's you'd notice. He didn't seem to scare you very much."

" He did his best," I said.

" He is rather crude," she said. " I think he was looking for something."

I must have looked as blank as I felt for she went on, " You don't know what I'm talking about, do you?"

" It would help a bit if you'd explain," I said. " He's welcome to what I've got. Apart from my money, that is. I only brought bathing trunks."

" I know," she said. " I looked already."

She smiled again. " There wouldn't be much point in going into details if we're at cross-purposes."

I thought for a moment. " If you and Otto are on the same side I think you're missing out," I said. " The rough and the smooth. I must say I prefer your technique to Otto though."

" I didn't say that," she said.

" Let's level, shall we?" I said. " Just what are you after? And just what was Mr. Grosvenor carrying that's so important to you and your friends?"

That hit home. She coloured up and looked confused for a second or two.

" If you think you can come in here and offer me a lazy lay you've chosen the wrong man," I said. " Not that I'm averse to a prettily-turned ankle. But I'm tired, it's hot as all hell and if we've got nothing to say to one another but verbal clichés I'll say goodnight. But if you want to lay your cards on the table, Miss Morris, instead of your can on the bed-clothes we can do business."

Her eyes looked at me levelly as she flicked the ash off her cigarette. " Always the gentleman," she said. " Sorry, I can't take you up on that."

" Then there's really nothing else to say," I said.

She hesitated. " Some other time."

I didn't know what the hell she was talking about. " Surely," I said. " And now you must excuse me."

I got hold of the bed-clothes and ripped them back. I don't know what I expected but it was a real eye-opener. She was stark naked under the bed-clothes and she didn't care who knew it. At least as far as I could see and that was around the waist. I didn't look any farther. She had excellent skin and everything else to go with it. She looked at me calmly and finished drawing at her cigarette.

" Nice tan," I said mechanically.

" You were saying?" she said.

I put back the bed-clothes reluctantly but firmly. " I think it's time you were on your way," I said.

Her eyes flickered. " You disappoint me, Mr. Faraday."

" I'm sorry, too," I said. " But we haven't been formally introduced. Besides, these walls are too thin."

She chuckled throatily. " I take back what I said earlier. You have the makings of a gentleman. The offer's only open for a limited period."

" I'll take a rain check on it," I said. I was standing now, quite close to the bed and she put up her face very quickly and kissed me once, warmly, on the mouth.

" Look after yourself," she said softly. " There are some nasty characters around this island."

" Is this the treatment you give to all the customers?" I said lightly.

" Only the special ones," she said. " And I shouldn't be warning you like this, but I've taken a fancy to you."

" I thought it was something," I said. I fingered the place where she'd kissed me. I could feel it still, way down to my shoes. There was a swish as she turned back the bed-clothes. I pretended not to look in the dressing table mirror on the opposite side of the room. She put on the polka-dot bikini that she'd left on a chair on the other side of the bed. A cream silk dressing-gown covered that; I faced round again as she wriggled into a pair of mules. She stubbed out her cigarette in the ashtray on the bedside table and gave me a last smile.

" What do you do for a living when you're not lying in other people's beds?" I said.

" I don't do anything," she said. " I don't need to work."

" That's nice, too," I said. I watched her out. She didn't say good night. After the door shut behind her I locked it but the way this place was run any passing drunk with a toothpick could have made open house with my room. I had just got my pyjama trousers on when there came a tap on the door. I opened it a crack.

Diane Morris peeked in round the edge of the door. She looked my physique over with relish.

" My, you are virile," she said.

" Correspondence course," I said. " I get my muscles next week."

She grinned. " I just came back to tell you I'm in No. 27 down the hall."

" I know," I told her. " I looked it up yesterday." Her smile matched my own. When I heard the door of her own room finally close I locked the door of mine for the night and leaned against it while I finished my cigarette. Before getting into bed I wandered out on to the balcony. A dollar moon was riding high, picking out the fretted edges of the wavelets in front of the hotel.

A hairy-chested ape was still practising high-dives in the pool under an arc-light. As I watched he cut down smoothly from the top-most board and entered the water with the clean-cut action of a door-bolt rammed home; his feet were drawn after him through a slit in the water with hardly a ripple. I sighed and went back into the bedroom.

I stubbed out my cigarette in the tray next to Diane's and almost regretted my sudden attack of purity. When I got into bed I had a job in sleeping properly; I could smell that damn perfume all night long and when I slept I dreamed that her head was next to mine. I woke in the night. There was no sound but the muffled chumble of the sea; I turned the pillow over to get rid of some of the scent and after that I slept better.

2

Next morning I was stopped in the lobby when I went in to breakfast. The manager called me over to the little cubby-hole on one side of the main reception desk that served him as an office. He handed me a buff-coloured envelope addressed to me in a scrawling inked handwriting that I didn't recognise.

" This came for you yesterday, Mr. Faraday," he said.

" Sorry, but I forgot to give it to you what with all the rumpus and everything."

" That's all right," I said, pushing it into an inside pocket of my jacket as I went in to meet Stella. I had only time to notice it had been posted in Stanley Bay a couple of days earlier.

I had arranged to go down there to see the Colonel along around mid-morning, so after I got Stella settled under a sun-shade out in front of the hotel, I went around to check on the Caddy. They had a big awning in back specially for guests' cars and after I had checked the radiator and the state of the gas I went on back up to my bedroom for a wash. I hadn't seen Diane but I had asked Stella to keep a discreet eye on her and let me know who she met and talked to during the day; but I hadn't told her why, of course. Clay hadn't shown for breakfast.

Now, back in the bedroom I put my coat over the back of a chair and indulged in the luxury of dousing my head in semi-cold water from the basin. I combed my hair and went out to the balcony; the railing was too hot for the hands so I stood back in the shade of the awning and looked out to sea. It was a beautiful morning and any other time I should have enjoyed the view but right now I had too much on my mind to be communing with nature.

I could see Stella lying partly under a striped umbrella; she had on a white two-piece. As I went to go back in I saw a familiar tawny-yellow mane on a girl just about to go in off the top diving board down at the pool. She had on an emerald-green one-piece sharkskin swimsuit and she streaked through the air in a perfect dive before easing herself almost gently into the water. It was Diane, but I hadn't noticed her before because I was looking for the wrong components.

She swam to the side of the pool in a couple of lazy strokes and shook the water from her hair in a casual movement which sent a shower of sparkling droplets in a wide circle about her. I looked from her to Stella and then back again. Nice as Diane was, Stella had the definite edge on her, I decided. Largely because she was unexplored territory, I suspected. I went on back into my room and was about to pick up my coat when I remembered the envelope.

I took it out and crackled it in my hand before opening it. I didn't know anyone here. It was decidedly curious. There wasn't any percentage in standing there so I tore the thing open. There was another enclosure inside, addressed to a woman in Chicago. I'll get to that in a moment. The letter, or note was written in crudely inked capitals in the same hand as the address on the main envelope. What made it memorable for me, though, was the wrapping on the message. I pulled out five C notes. In American currency too. This was nice payment for the fatigue of reading what was written on it. I hoped this was the beginning of a regular correspondence.

The letter was short and to the point. It said: MR. FARADAY, YOU WON'T KNOW ME BUT I READ YOUR NAME IN THE PAPERS. WHEN YOU GET BACK TO THE STATES PLEASE HAVE THE ENCLOSED LETTER DELIVERED PERSONALLY. I HOPE THE 500 DOLLARS WILL MAKE IT WORTH YOUR WHILE. J.M.

I sat down and lit a cigarette. I sat and smoked and looked at the note and the currency and the enclosure and it seemed to get hotter than ever.

" If this means what I think it does, you're a mean old bastard," I said to no-one in particular. But I was thinking of the man in the white drill suit and the red tie who was now lying in the down-town morgue. If he had posted the letter in Stanley Bay two afternoons ago someone might remember him. And he must have been picked up by the two friends in the row-boat a short while after. Something else for Colonel Clay to think about. The Ancient Mariner might remember something too.

After a little further thought I tore open the enclosure. It was addressed to a Mrs. J. Melissa at an address in West Side Chicago. I sat until my cigarette burned down nearly to my fingers. Things were beginning to add up. I thought I had what Diane's friends were looking for. It was time to see Colonel Clay. I went downstairs, had a few words with Stella before I came away and drove off down the coast to Stanley Bay.

For once I didn't notice the heat; the white dust of the road settled on the bonnet and drifted into the seats but I was so pre-occupied that I didn't even blast out a coloured man on an ancient green bicycle who shot out of a side road as I was getting near the town. Barney's call was due in around midday and it wasn't yet eleven, but my news would take a bit of chewing over. And I wanted to settle one or two things with Clay before I spoke to Barney.

I slid into a vacant lot outside the Stanley Bay Police Office, next to Clay's scarlet sports job and one of the big police trucks. I went on into the office. The same bored-looking sergeant was fly-swatting at his desk, another constable manned the telephone switchboard. The sergeant smiled and waved me on in. I knocked at Clay's door and when I heard him call out I walked through. Clay was sitting at his desk with Inspector Phillips by his side. They were looking at a map spread out in front of them. Clay got up as I came through the door.

" Sorry about breakfast," he said. " Something came up. Take a seat, Michael," he added cheerfully. " We were just closing shop on the deep-freeze plants."

Phillips got up with a smile and seemed about to excuse himself but Colonel Clay stopped him with a hand on his arm.

" I want you to stay, Ian," he said. " This concerns us all."

Phillips sat down again. Clay turned back to me. He buzzed for the sergeant and presently a constable brought in three coffees in plastic cups. The coffee was hot and tasted pretty good, judged by British standards.

" How did you make out?" I asked Clay. I was referring to the case in general terms but he got my message. I looked out of the window at the big yacht riding in the bay. He shook his head.

" No movement there for the moment. We haven't disturbed them—yet."

" Anything on the deep-freeze angle?" I asked.

Phillips nodded. " We found very slight traces of frozen blood on the floor under the ice. It was so minute the men who committed the murder—and Dr. Griffith has conclusively proved that—overlooked it. On analysis it matches up with Grosvenor's group."

" That just about sews it up," I said. " Except for Henaway." I was referring to the labourer at the Cucumber Cay deep-freeze plant.

Clay shook his head again. " We haven't turned him up yet. It may take a few days."

I looked out again to where *The Gay Lady* swung with the tide.

" It must be getting pretty crowded aboard there," I said. The Colonel smiled thinly.

" An assumption but a fairly logical one," he said. " We hadn't overlooked that possibility."

" Did you question Long John Silver?" I asked.

Clay knotted his brows and then broke into a short laugh.

" You mean the dockside philosopher?" he said. " That's Stan Travis. He's a local character. Garrulous and a perfect pest but pretty harmless. He thinks he might be able to identify one of the two men who took Grosvenor out fishing."

" What about the boat-hire people?" I asked.

It was Phillips' turn to smile. " The boat was hired by phone in the name of Jones," he said.

" Not very inventive, are they?" I said. " So?"

" They picked the boat up in the lunch-hour when the operator had closed up and gone for a meal," said Phillips. " They came back late and left the hire-money with Travis. Apparently he looks after things for the odd tip when the owner is away."

" So the boat-hire people didn't see the two men at all," I said. " Convenient."

" Fortunately," said the Colonel, " the boat hadn't been used since. We went for a ride this morning."

I said nothing. Clay went on, " Ian had a bright idea. He measured the fuel in the tank. Then we filled up and took a trip out to Cucumber Cay and back. The amount of fuel used just about matched that in the tank when the two men brought the boat back. And it had been full when the hire-period began."

I looked admiringly at Clay and then back to Phillips.

" It's a pleasure to work with you gentlemen," I said.

Then it was my play. I threw down the envelope and the enclosure on Clay's desk.

" From a Mr. Melissa," I said. " It's my belief that he and Grosvenor add up to the same party."

Clay looked surprised. He read the note, examined the envelope and the money, passed them to Phillips and then took up the second envelope and the enclosure. He put it one one side and paused long enough to ask me a question.

As a matter of interest where would he have heard your name ?"

I lit a cigarette. Clay leaned across the desk to light it for me. I stared out of the window across at *The Gay Lady*.

" He comes from Chicago," I said. " The papers were full of this Washington espionage business a month or two ago. I wasn't exactly inconspicuous at that time."

The Colonel nodded. " I see. He may well have seen your photograph."

" And anyone could have read my name in the hotel

register," I said. " We didn't come incognito. And he had a room only one flight above us."

The Colonel spread out the single sheet of paper the second stamped envelope had contained. On the uppermost side was written in the same capitals as the message to me : JANET—PUT THIS IN A SAFE PLACE.

There was no signature, nothing else. On the reverse of the sheet was a drawing; it consisted of little else but grid lines. Across the surface of the sheet were scattered small groups of figures; 7, 14, 12, 10 and so on. Near the bottom of the sheet was a number of groups of figures and letters.

" What do you make of this, Michael?" said the Colonel.

" Looks like some sort of map-reference," I said guardedly. " This isn't really my strong point."

The Colonel stroked his chin. " Shouldn't be too difficult," he said. " It's obviously a map tracing of an area somewhere near this island. The small figures representing soundings in fathoms. The other groups are the bearing of something in latitude and longitude."

Phillips grinned. " Hidden treasure, sir?"

The Colonel shot him a humorous glance. " And why not, my boy?" he said. " You're getting too cynical. I think we've got something important here."

" But it isn't much use without the actual chart," I said.

The Colonel clicked his teeth with the nearest thing to annoyance I had seen since I knew him.

" Simplest thing in the world," he said. " This is a tracing. We can soon match it up in the standard book of charts. The soundings alone make identification relatively simple. Of course, the actual bearings may be in code or scrambled or otherwise transposed. But we have people who can soon break that down."

He sat down at his desk again, his eyes shining like a boy who'd found an unattended candy stall.

" Let's hear your theory, Michael."

" Grosvenor or Melissa wanted to hide something and chose me as the messenger," I said. " He posted the letter but the opposition got to him soon afterwards. Sixty-four dollar question is what the prize is. Barney may help there. But ten to one the answer's on that yacht."

Colonel Clay's eyes looked half asleep as he screwed up his face against the sun spilling in at the window.

" I'm inclined to agree with you," he said. " We shall know soon enough if your Chicago friend is up to his job What's your idea on all this, Ian ?"

Phillips shifted uncomfortably in his chair. " I haven't really given it much thought at the moment, sir. A robbery perhaps. Or thieves fallen out ? I'm inclined to think that the hidden object might not be money at all. There's the practical difficulty of Grosvenor carting currency or securities out here with him. He flew in from the States and the Customs checks are pretty stringent. We've heard nothing from that end, remember."

The Colonel leaned back in his chair. " A good point, Ian," he said. " I must confess I hadn't worked that one out myself. The probability seems to point to a document which might give directions to the whereabouts of an item of value."

" There is another thing, sir," said Phillips after a short silence. " And that in turn depends on the map reference, as to whether the location of the object is on land—that is, on an island—or whether it's under the sea."

The Colonel and I exchanged glances; this was getting entertaining. Clay looked at his watch.

" A quarter to twelve," he said. " We'd better stand by for your call, Michael." He nodded to Phillips. " I should get busy on the charts, Ian, if I were you. Make a copy of that drawing first and give me back the original. I'll put that in the safe and make sure of it. Let me know if you get stuck."

Phillips put on his cap and said, " I'll be up in the

Records Office, sir, if you want me." He smiled at me, saluted and went out.

Clay got up, glanced at his watch again and took me by the arm. I followed him into the outer room. I had a momentary pang. I'd said nothing so far about Diane Morris. I was keeping her in reserve. Whether for myself or for the Colonel's information I wasn't quite sure. But if I told him then I had to let Stella in too. And I didn't want to spoil her holiday. Or mine for that matter. I walked over to the switchboard.

3

I sat and talked into the phone while Barney listened. Colonel Clay stood in front of the switchboard. The sergeant and two constables gathered in a semi-circle while the constable at the switchboard sat with his fingers tensed nervously, worried in case the link might be broken. I told Barney the set-up as we knew it; what we had discovered, what we thought might be behind it. I could feel Clay fidgeting as the minutes ticked by.

When I stopped Barney started. I'd picked a good man. He'd got all the information we wanted. I beckoned to the sergeant and he slid a note-pad across the table to me. I jotted down a few facts as Barney went on.

"Johnny Melissa," I said, scribbling. "That figures." I whistled at his next piece of information. That made the whole thing jell. "What about the little guy?" I asked.

"You were right again," said Barney. "Joe Scarpini. Usually works with a big fellow built like the side of a house."

"We've met," I said. "Otto mean anything to you?"

"Otto Schultz," he said. He sounded surprised. "Looks like you got yourself a Chicago Convention out there."

I got busy with the pad again as he went on. I remembered the little man now; Scarpini. I hadn't any special reason to recall his name but I figured that quite a lot of people in Chicago had. He was real mean.

" You'll let us know if you come up with anything, won't you?" said Barney. " The City of Chicago has a personal interest in most of that money."

" We're working on it," I said. " I wanted to check with you first. The English police can't move without a warrant and there was no sense in alarming these birds. Looks like you can scrub Melissa off your records. Just a question of time before we break the map reference. But there's a lot of difference between proof and suspicion. If we tip our hand too soon these characters will take off. And there's nothing we can do about it."

I could see Barney nodding to himself at the other end of the phone. I gave him a description of Lloyd, the man who owned *The Gay Lady*.

" That doesn't ring a bell," he said. " Could fit anybody. But the name means nothing. Have you checked on the yacht registration?" I repeated the question to Clay.

" We sent to Nassau," he said. " We still haven't had a reply."

He sounded aggrieved, like I'd caught him out in a gross piece of inefficiency. I finished off the call by telling Barney that I'd check out with him in a couple of days. Clay nodded to indicate that he would lay it on again for midday. As I finished Ian Phillips came down a staircase on the other side of the room waving a piece of paper and smiling. He quietened down as Clay shot him a warning glance. I thanked Barney and rang off.

" I got this position pin-pointed," Phillips broke in enthusiastically.

" And I got news for you," I told Clay.

" Before we do anything else we'll go back in the office," he said primly. The sergeant turned back to his desk and the little group round the switchboard broke up with exaggerated haste and started bustling about the office.

Clay led the way back into his own room. When we had all settled ourselves the Colonel said, " I see you've had a profitable call, Michael."

" The news is this," I said. " Johnny Melissa, the real name of this Grosvenor character, was the treasurer of the Chicago branch of the Mafia. The word is that he left town with their life savings."

The Colonel blew out his breath with a sudden, sharp explosive sound. Ian Phillips sat staring at me for a moment before he remembered himself and shut his mouth with a snap.

" Did they say any amount?" said Clay at last.

" The figure mentioned was somewhere around a quarter of a million dollars," I said.

The Colonel blinked. " That's about £85,000 in real money," he explained to Phillips.

" A sizeable piece of change in any language," I said. " Enough to get Grosvenor killed anyways."

The Colonel turned back to me. " So his colleagues followed him out here and finished him off," he said.

" But without finding where he'd stashed the money," I said. " That ties in Otto Schultz and Scarpini. Mr. Lloyd and *The Gay Lady* could bear some looking into."

" Probably an alias," said Phillips.

" I daresay," said Clay. " They obviously haven't found out where the money is or they'd have made a move before now. Where was that map reference, by the way, Ian?"

" Place about ten miles up the coast, sir," said Phillips. " Not very deep water but a mile or two off shore."

" Which means that the money isn't there," I said. " He probably dropped a waterproof package over secured to an underwater marker."

" The contents giving information on the whereabouts of the cash," said the Colonel approvingly. " Most ingenious."

"A safe deposit box, a bank or some hideout in the States," I said. "I think we can leave that to Uncle Sam once we locate it."

Phillips was frowning. "Question is, did Melissa have an accomplice or is he a navigation expert? I mean, whoever plotted this position must have been pretty good or he'd never find what he'd dropped overboard."

"Believe it or not, Melissa served for a period in the U.S. Navy during the war," I said. "He was a navigation officer aboard a battleship until they caught him misappropriating the ship's funds. Even then there was a considerable sum involved. He was dismissed the service and sent to gaol for six months."

Clay rubbed his hands. "It all seems pretty clear-cut," he said. "The only trouble is we haven't a scrap of proof against these people on the yacht. That's where you come in, Michael."

"I was hoping you'd say that," I said.

Phillips grinned and Clay permitted himself a shadow of a smile.

"What I can't see, sir, is why we don't just sort these people out," said Phillips. "At the moment we're sitting here and they're sitting out there in a sort of stalemate."

"I've already partly answered that," Clay told him. "If we go off half-cock on this thing there's nothing to prevent *The Gay Lady* sailing once we lift the ban. And we can't hold all these people up more than another day or two. We've still got about fifty boats to check."

"I think I'll have to pay an informal call before then," I said.

"We don't know that, officially," Clay said, intently studying the ceiling of the office.

"Check," I said. "Which is why I shall leave your police authorisation with you for the time being."

I took the document out of my wallet and handed it to Phillips; he passed it over on to Clay's blotter.

" Very diplomatic, Michael," the Colonel went on. " We can't afford to get mixed up in any unofficial proceedings. But we'll give you every help in an undercover way."

" I thought I might take a trip some time tonight," I said. " We could go over it later this afternoon if you've got time." Clay nodded and got to his feet as I stood up.

" I can't persuade you to stay to lunch, I suppose?"

" Thanks, but I'd better get back to the Catamaran," I said. " I've been neglecting Stella the last day or two."

" I'm free, sir," said Phillips brightly.

" You won't have time," Clay told him crisply, " with all the paper work I'm just going to give you."

Phillips chuckled as I went on out. As I went through the door Clay called, " Give my regards to the young lady."

" Right. Back about four," I said. Outside, I put on some dark glasses I'd bought earlier in the week. They made me look like something out of a B gangster movie, but they were necessary; driving is hard on the eyes in these parts. I got into the Caddy and tooled gently along the jetty, past the painted backdrop of the harbour with its sea-shimmer and soon left the tarmac roads behind. Once outside Stanley Bay the country became rugged and primitive, with stone outcrops, green scrub, palms and thick vegetation which came down close on to the dusty road.

I had gone about two miles when I came on a big blue sedan parked at the side of the road; a girl was bending over the open bonnet and one of the car doors was open. I went by in a swirl of dust before I realised that she hadn't parked but was in trouble. I started reversing and she looked up and waved as I got closer. There was some-thing familiar about her and then I recognised Diane Morris.

CHAPTER SEVEN

Mr. Mandrake

I

SHE WAS wearing a cream linen suit and there was a warm flush to her face. She bent over the bonnet of the car with an exasperated expression and then straightened up as she heard the Caddy coming back. I saw a thin smear of oil on her forehead; she was already patting her hair into place. I stopped the motor, set the handbrake and got out of the driving seat.

" Having trouble?" I said.

She smiled. " Sort of."

I walked across the few yards that separated us.

" Perhaps I can help."

" Not unless you make a better score than you done so far," said a third voice. A big, beefy figure materialised on the other side of the sedan; there was a smaller figure beside him. It was Otto, the bedroom midget and his sidekick. He didn't have his gun out. He didn't have to.

" That's the last time I stop for a lady," I said to no-one in particular.

Diane Morris flushed. She bit her lip, looked as if she was about to say something, then slammed the bonnet shut viciously and busied herself fixing her face in a wing mirror.

" That's the truth, snooper," said Scarpini seriously. " 'Cept she ain't no lady."

" What can I do for you boys?" I said.

" We'd like to take a little trip together," said the one Diane Morris had called Otto.

" Supposing I don't want to go?" I said.

Otto shrugged. " Won't make no difference," he said simply. Very likely. He had a good point there.

" What's this all about?" I asked.

" Mr. Mandrake wants to see you," Otto said.

" The name means nothing to me," I said.

Scarpini sniggered.

" He knows all about you," he said to Diane Morris' back, biting off his words with care, like they cost him a dime a time. Otto walked around the car and opened the rear door on my side.

" It's a nice afternoon for exercise," he observed. " Coming?"

" Why not," I said. " It's too hot for gymnastics and I got my best suit on."

He laughed. Scarpini looked disappointed and took his hand out of his pocket. He went around to the driving seat of my Caddy and stood waiting. I threw him the keys. He caught them with an expert back flip of his hand, got in the car, started up the engine and turned her around. He came on back towards us and sat with the engine idling.

Diane Morris got in the driving seat of the blue sedan; I got in back and the big fellow got in beside me. I noted that the door catch of the nearside rear door was in the locked position. Not that it would have made any difference. Otto had his hand in his pocket and his eyes didn't miss a trick. Diane started up the engine, turned the big car in a perfect three-point movement and softly idled down the track in front of Scarpini, who had stayed behind in the Caddy. We drove back down the road towards Stanley Bay.

D

I kept silent and the big fellow didn't look in a talkative mood; nothing was alive in his face except his eyes and they followed my slightest movement.

" Mind if I smoke ?" I asked.

He nodded. " But take it easy. Make it real slow."

I reached carefully for a pack in my pocket. I put the cigarette between my lips. He already had a match lit. He held it to the tip of the cigarette. The flame burned rock-steady.

" Thanks," I said and blew it out. He put the burned-out match in the ashtray on the back of the front seat. All the while his eyes never left my face.

I could see Diane reflected in the big visor mirror set in the centre of the windshield. She kept her face down towards the road but she looked worried. Occasionally she bit her lip. We all three acted like it was a funeral. That was another sobering thought. We went through the out-skirts of Stanley Bay. She drove slowly, never more than twenty miles an hour; there wasn't much percentage, with these sort of roads, but even when she hit tarmac she didn't increase the speed.

The big sedan went right through the centre of town. When the Police Office started coming up I looked in the mirror and saw Scarpini had stopped my car farther back along the jetty. He slotted it in near the Harbour Master's office. He got out quickly, glanced around and then walked off. We went on past the Police H.Q. and just when I thought we were about to take a nose-dive off the end of the jetty, she throttled down to a crawl and turned the car at right angles and I saw something I hadn't noticed before.

There was a long stone-flagged walk which continued the harbour; it looked like the older part of Stanley Bay. There was hardly room for two cars to pass but the whole purpose of the manoeuvre was the high screen of buttonwood, sapodillo and mastic trees which fringed this part of the quay. These, with the palmettos at the back effectively hid our arrival from Colonel Clay and the other occupants of the Stanley Bay Police Office.

Diane tooled the sedan to a gentle stop right up against a high stone wall; she pulled in so close we had to get out on the opposite side of the car.

" No tricks, mind," Otto breathed at me softly as he backed out his door. He stood facing me, his broad body seeming to block out most of the panorama of the harbour. A moment later Scarpini re-joined us from the other end of the jetty; he must have cut across a back way to avoid the Police Office. We didn't have long to wait. We had hardly got out of the car before the putt-putt of an outboard motor reached us and a large dinghy came in from the big yacht out in mid-harbour.

It put in smartly at the bottom of the ladder and Scarpini caught the painter which was thrown up to him by the helmsman; he was the only man in the boat. A small, good-humoured looking Chinaman with gap teeth. He was dressed in a white sweat shirt that looked like someone had been wiping his boots on it and his jeans had seen better days too. I got down the ladder and into the stern of the boat. Scarpini, the girl and Otto followed. The Chinaman gave me an ear-splitting grin. " Welcome to *Gay Lady*, mlistah," he said in a high-pitched voice and immediately went off into a shrill, whinnying laugh.

" You'd be a natural for Saturday-night TV programmes," I told him. He tittered again, then revved up the motor as he put the tiller over; Otto shoved off at the stern and we headed out from the jetty back to the yacht.

Diane Morris sat down in the bow on a bench near Scarpini who sat and watched me; Otto came down into the stern and sat across from me and watched both me and the steersman.

" This here's Charley Fong," he said, jerking his head at the Chinese, who broke out one of his grins again.

" He does the cooking aboard, such as it is."

He spat reflectively overside; I didn't know whether the gesture was a comment on the cooking or not, but it didn't seem to bother Mr. Fong any. I thought his lips were going to meet round the back of his neck.

We rounded the yacht a short while afterwards; there was a small chop running here and we shipped a spoonful or two of water over the bow as the little man ran the boat alongside *The Gay Lady*. She was a bigger vessel than I had thought and her sheer towered a long way above us. Charley Fong throttled the motor back and it died to a throaty chuckle, re-echoed by the slap of the exhaust on the water as he tooled the boat in to a teak and brass ladder, a swell affair, that led up to the deck of the yacht.

Scarpini tied up the bow of the boat to the ladder and we all got off and went up on deck; Scarpini led, Diane Morris followed, then I went up and Otto and the China-man fetched up the rear.

Up here there was a welcome breeze to dilute the heat of the sun; I could see the whole curve of the harbour and Stanley Bay, particularly the Union Jack fluttering from the flagpole outside the Police Office. I wondered if Clay knew I was aboard; I could imagine the scene if Phillips was busy with his binoculars.

I stepped down off the gangway on to the wide planking of the deck; the yacht was beautifully kept. The timbers were scrubbed white, the teak rail shone with fresh varnish; even the lanyard lashing on the canvas covers of the ship's boats was pipe-clayed. I could smell money; it spoke in the gleaming brass fittings, in the stainless steel rigging and above all the wheelhouse.

Through the broad, glassed windows I could see a radar set and all the latest navigational gear; somewhere a generator whined and there was a faint compound in the air that you only get aboard such a vessel—a subtle blend of salt, diesel oil and champagne. Scarpini led the way amidships and we went down a wide companionway, ducking under a canvas cover. Here the deck fittings were re-echoed in teak and mahogany; the overhead deck lights winked on brass and chrome. The corridor carpet was a good inch thick.

We trod noiselessly on as we walked for about a block and a half until Scarpini brought up against a pair of big sliding doors. They went back almost noiselessly, in perfectly oiled and carpentered runners. He waved us through. We were in a large saloon that must have occupied most of the upper midships of the yacht. It was about fifty feet long and twenty wide. Scarlet carpeting made a vivid lawn of the deck under our feet; leather divans of a dull mushroom colour spread along under the wide panoramic windows which surrounded us on three sides.

A vivid wedge of blue sky shone down through deckhead hatches in the middle of the mahogany panelled ceiling; a crystal chandelier depended from a big beam which ran transversely across the centre of the saloon. It was braced and protected by disguised cables running into the deckhead, which repeated the motif of the chandelier itself.

Charley Fong had disappeared somewhere but Scarpini was still with us; he went and sat on one of the leather divans and played with a fruit knife he picked up off one of the tables as we went by. There was a colossal bar let into one side of the room; everything in it was fiddled and strutted to prevent bottles and glasses from flying about in heavy weather.

At the far end of the saloon, at the bow end of the boat where the big windows made a kind of windscreen backed by distant views of the harbour, was an alcove. It was surrounded on three sides by the saloon windows and fringed by three enormous divans; these were of black leather. They surrounded a large and highly polished mahogany table which was secured to the deck by heavy brass fittings at the foot.

Fans moved silently in fixed arcs from their positions on the bulkhead every eight feet or so. They only succeeded in re-distributing the torpid air. The coolness came from the breeze which filtered in from the half-opened panoramic windows.

One of the features of the saloon was the set of heavy duty glass fish tanks set about the room. There were four in all. Two in the bulkheads, one each side of the saloon. These were mainly for effect. They had fluorescent lighting inside and I had to admit they made an attractive Jules Verne study from a seated position. It would be even better at night, giving the viewer the impression he was in a submarine.

There were two other tanks set down the saloon, right about where the centre of stability would have been. These were of thicker glass than the others. They were taller too, and the water came only about three quarters of the way up their sides. The tops were closed over with specially designed vents which would admit air but would prevent water from slopping out of them when the ship was under way in rough weather.

The owner didn't want to spoil his carpets, I guess. I didn't blame him. These last tanks had only a few small fish in them; they looked like tropical specimens. I was disappointed. It looked hardly worth the trouble of such elaborate tanks. I would have expected twelve-foot eels for that sort of money.

But just at the moment it was the man seated in the big alcove at the end of the saloon who occupied my attention. He was a remarkable specimen.

2

Mr. Mandrake was a big, chunky box of a man. His short blond hair was cropped close to his blunt skull and stuck up like bristles all over his head. His skin was a delicate pink but that was the only delicate thing about him. His eyes were wide-spaced, pale-grey and quite expressionless but the long blond eye-lashes, almost feminine in their length, contrasted in a startling manner with the greyness of his eyes and the pinkness of his skin.

He had the blunt chin and the big nose of a boxer; his mouth was wide with deep lines round the corners and when he smiled, which wasn't often, he revealed strong, irregular yellow teeth. An incised scar about two inches long which ran diagonally from a point above his left eyebrow ended among the roots of his blond hair and made a white gash against the lobster shade of his complexion.

When he stood up as we got close to the table I was surprised to see that he was comparatively short in stature; it was his breadth and the general scale on which he was built which had given me an impression of size. His age could have been anything from thirty-five to fifty-five. His bulky frame was encased in an impeccably cut grey silk suit with shawl lapels. He wore a wide-collared shirt of stunning whiteness, and a pale-yellow bow tie with tiny red motifs on it that I couldn't make out.

His hands were chunky; the big fingers thick as cigars, but the nails were well kept. There was the glint of a gold watch on one wrist and a handkerchief which made the detergent ads look positively dingy peeped from the breast pocket of his jacket. His hands were pink too and they looked like starfish clusters against the sober background of his suit. He stared at me hard for a moment.

"So glad you could come, Mr. Faraday." His hand was hard, cool and dry. I couldn't place his accent. The hand-shake was about as sincere as a Rotarian's weekly lunch-smile. He waved one of the star-fish around and indicated the divan behind the table.

"Do sit down."

I remained standing. Scarpini moved at my side. He

clamped his hand over my arm and pushed downwards.

" You heard what Mr. Mandrake said," he gritted.

" Go pull the chain and flush yourself out," I told him. I moved sideways and then Scarpini came up with the fruit knife. Mr. Mandrake moved then, with astonishing rapidity for a man of such a big build.

The pink starfish of his hand described a dazzling curve in the air. There was a sharp crunch of bone meeting flesh and Scarpini flew from one side of the cabin to the other. The fruit knife shot from his hand and Otto quickly put a foot on it. Scarpini got up. He was breathing heavily and the expression on his face wasn't friendly. A white line spread diagonally across his face where Mandrake had cracked him and a thin trickle of blood ran from the corner of his nose.

" Get out," Mandrake told him evenly. " This is no time for rough stuff. And take the pig-sticker with you."

There was such authority in his voice that Scarpini just seemed to melt away; Otto handed him the knife blade first. There was a grin on his face. The girl hadn't moved. Otto went and sat on the other end of the horse-shoe divan. Mandrake waved his hand again.

" I must apologise Mr. Faraday. But one must take the hired help one can get. Won't you sit down—please."

I sat down near him behind the big mahogany table and fished for a cigarette. He came up with a silver embossed box from the table. The cigarettes were a foreign brand, with little coronets stencilled on the tubes, and tasted lousy enough to be very expensive. He leaned forward and flourished a silver lighter in his big pink hand. I lit the cigarette from it and sat back on the cushions and feathered the smoke at the skylight.

" How did you know my name?" I asked him. It was pretty obvious how since it had been down in the Catamaran guest book for everyone to see but I was just curious to hear his reply.

" It is not unknown in the wider world," he said. " But I am neglecting my duties as host. A drink, perhaps. Will you do the honours, my dear."

Diane Morris got up from her end of the divan and went over to the cocktail cabinet. Mandrake cocked his eyebrows at me.

" Since this is purely a social visit I'll have a planter's punch," I said.

Mr. Mandrake smiled thinly, revealing his irregular teeth. " An excellent choice in this climate," he said. " Make that two, my dear."

He looked across at Otto.

" Bourbon—with plenty of ice."

Diane Morris mixed the drinks and handed them round. I noticed she had bourbon also, with not too much seltzer. Then she went and sat on the end of the divan again and clinked the ice in her goblet with a long glass mixing rod. Mandrake sat drinking without saying anything. He seemed inordinately interested in studying the tips of his brown suède sneakers. He wore grey silk socks too, I noted. I figured I'd make a good high fashion spy if I was ever sent to cover a mannequin parade. I put out my cigarette in a large gimballed ashtray on one side of the table and made a hole in my drink. Diane had mixed it well and the rum tasted real good.

Mandrake set his drink down with a sigh and folded his pink hands across one knee. " Now let's get down to business, Mr. Faraday. Would 5,000 dollars interest you?"

I blinked. " Would I be interested in going on breathing?" I said. " What do I have to do? Assassinate the governor?"

Mandrake chuckled throatily. " Nothing so melodramatic —or so profitless, I can assure you. We are merely looking for a piece of information. I think you can help us."

He stopped for a moment, picked up his glass and looked stonily at me over the rim of it.

" I shall expect quite a lot of information for 5,000 dollars," he said. " Accurate information."

" Never welshed on a client yet," I said. " No information, no fee."

" It is not quite so simple as that, Mr. Faraday," he continued. " A man has been killed on the island. You know all about that, of course."

" A Mr. Grosvenor," I said innocently. " I could hardly avoid hearing about it since we were both checked in at the same hotel."

Mandrake nodded. " Quite so," he said. " Mr. Grosvenor had something belonging to us. And I want it back. I am willing to pay you the 5,000 dollars to get it for me. Since you are already a guest at the Catamaran you are in a good position to do so without attracting too much attention. My men are altogether too conspicuous."

" You can say that again," I said. " Junior here was trying to be rather forceful the other evening."

Otto shifted uncomfortably and buried his head in his glass. Mr. Mandrake sighed. " With little effect," he said. " Now that I have met you I can see just how foolish and ill-advised a move that was. But you see the sort of associates with which I am surrounded. It is difficult to do much without using such men, but their efforts are inevitably crude and pointless."

" Except in the case of Mr. Grosvenor," I said.

There was a deep silence. Mr. Mandrake lifted his eyebrows. " Indeed?" he said. " Would you mind explaining?"

" The ice gag," I said. " What was the alibi?"

Mr. Mandrake smiled slowly. Too thinly and without too much sincerity.

" You are a man after my own heart, Mr. Faraday. I must congratulate myself on my choice. Without admitting anything, I was at the Stanley Bay Yacht Club all the afternoon in question. In a prominent position on the verandah, surrounded by the local worthies. I think even the local police chief would find that hard to crack."

I looked at him for a long moment and then drained my glass. Diane Morris was at my elbow. She took the glass from me and I heard the clink of ice-cubes as she started to re-fill it.

" Since we are being so frank, Mr. Faraday," said Mr. Mandrake. " I think it is your turn to answer some questions."

I leaned back against the cushions. " Fire away," I said.

" You seem altogether too friendly with the local police force," he said. " That will have to stop if we are to be associated."

" I was only assisting them with their inquiries," I said. " As far as I can make out they haven't turned up a thing so far. It would look kinda odd if they were suddenly socially unacceptable. Besides, it's going to be difficult to me to operate if I'm not to contact them. And I shall have to rely on them for information, if I'm going to find what you're looking for. What are you looking for, anyway?"

A frown chased across Mandrake's face. He looked out through the big windows at the blues and greens of the harbour.

" We don't really know," he said. " It'll probably be nothing more than a piece of paper with some information on it. It might be in code; concealed in a letter—or in any one of half a dozen ways. That's your job. I should start with Grosvenor's room."

" I thought your girl friend would have been there already," I said.

He looked over at Diane Morris. She flushed but said nothing. Then he laughed again. " She didn't make too good a job of it either," he said. " As I said, all my help can't avoid attracting attention. That's where you come in."

" Police have already been over it," I said. " They didn't find anything."

"Amateurs," he said. "It needs a trained man. I want you to give that room the whole works."

"All right," I said. "You might have something."

He looked me straight in the face again. "And, Mr. Faraday, just remember one thing. Play square with us. I'm sure I don't have to make myself more explicit. There's a lot of money involved here."

"There must be to sweeten me up with 5,000 iron men," I said.

He sipped again at his drink. "See that you earn it," he said.

He beckoned to Otto. The big man passed over a leather brief-case he took from a shelf behind the divan. Mandrake rummaged around in the case and came up with a big bundle of notes.

He counted out ten, all brand new, and threw them across to me.

"A thousand on account," he said. "Better check them to make sure."

"You want a receipt for these?" I asked him.

"I don't think that will be necessary," Mandrake said blandly.

"I knew a guy like you once," I said. "He was so rich he even had the inside of his Rolls wall-papered."

Diane Morris smiled for the first time since we met that afternoon. I put the wad of notes into my wallet and then put that back into my inside pocket. It seemed to burn a hole in the lining.

Mandrake got to his feet. "And now that we have concluded our business, let me show you the yacht."

He led the way down the centre of the saloon. Otto sat still on the divan except that he'd slightly changed his position so that his eyes could watch my every move. Diane came over from the hooch stall. She handed me another long glass. Her fingers brushed mine for just a short while longer than was strictly necessary. I raised the glass and drank to her. She smiled again. Mandrake was standing by one of the big central fish-tanks.

" Are you interested in tropical fish, Mr. Faraday?" he asked.

" Not particularly," I said.

" A pity. A most fascinating study."

He tapped the glass of the tank and the fish inside milled around uneasily. They were only small things, about four inches long, a silver grey velvet colour with tiny gold flecks. Their fan-like tails parted the water lazily. Their little red eyes looked blandly and innocently out at us. There was only one thing I didn't like about them—or two to be strictly accurate. The little white barbs which stuck up each side of their mouths; when they gulped, which they did occasionally, rows of minute white teeth made ivory patterns in their gullets.

" Do you know what these are?" said Mandrake almost dreamily. He tapped the side of the tank again and the little fish went round in a vivid circle. I shook my head.

" They are of the species Serrasalmus," he said. " From South America. Or, to a layman like yourself they may be familiar under their more common name of Piranha."

I shrugged. " Aren't they supposed to be the little fellows that can tear a guy to strips in about nothing flat?"

He smiled. " A slight exaggeration of the popular cinema, the penny novelette and the comic strip. They can be dangerous, yes, especially when encountered *en masse* in their native rivers. They usually go for cattle, seldom man. Blood is their primary motivation—an open cut or wound would be fatal. These are quite harmless for the moment."

Then he did something which got me. He lifted off the vent and plunged one of his pink hands down into the green water. The little fish circled gingerly and then drew back. He waved his hand through the water, following a particular fish; when it stopped near the end of the tank he gently scratched its flank. It let him do it for a moment and then slid away. He just stood there looking at me. I felt sweat trickle down my collar. After about a million years he took his hand out again. He laughed.

" You see, quite harmless. Would you like to try ?"

" No thanks," I said. " I wouldn't look good with a metal hook."

He laughed again and the tension in the saloon relaxed.

" The explanation is perfectly simple. No blood and, of course, these fish are well fed. Raw meat and such-like, you know. If there had been a cut on my hand it would have been a different story."

He led the way over to the second tank. " In contrast, these fish have not been fed for some time. There is quite a difference. In fact, I would not advise anyone putting their hand into this one."

" Don't get your tanks mixed up," I told him.

He sat down in a deep leather armchair. " There is not much fear of that, Mr. Faraday."

Just then we were interrupted by a curious noise. Mr. Mandrake looked up sharply. It came from Otto. He had gotten up on to the divan. Foam came from his mouth and flecked his clothing. His voice, when it came, was a shrill scream.

" Get that damn thing outta here," he yelled. Something I hadn't seen before loped down the room; it was an ordinary white cat with pink albino eyes, but it had a fantastic effect upon Otto. He almost went up in the air. His hand plucked at his clothing, and the Luger came up, its black snout looking like the barrel of a cannon as he waved it at us.

" That damn Charley Fong," he raved. " I told him to keep that thing outta my way or I'd murder it."

Mr. Mandrake stood up then very suddenly. His voice cracked like a whip. " Drop it Otto, do you hear ?"

The cat came on down the room, picking its way between the furniture with mincing steps. It seemed to sense the big man's fear and made straight for the divan. Something black went through the air and hit Otto's gun hand and spun him off balance. The leather cushion Mandrake had thrown, tumbled on the carpet and with it the Luger Otto had the good sense to drop.

The big man screamed as the cat jumped at him; it clawed at his face and he went over on the divan in a mêlée of arms and legs. The cat yowled once as the big man's hand caught it and then it had dug its claws into the calf of his leg. Otto seemed to go raving mad then. With a hoarse shriek he swung his foot, crashed the cat's body against the arm of the divan and then, half-dazed, it released its hold and was flung through the air towards Mandrake. It bounced against the leg of the big tank against which we were sitting and landed on the carpet spitting viciously. Blood glistened on its flank.

Before anyone could move Mandrake had it by the scruff of the neck; he pulled the vent of the big tank off with a quick wrench of his disengaged hand and then he held the spitting cat down into the suddenly agitated water.

A thin scream that fretted our nerves like jets of boiling water came from the cat; the liquid in the tank foamed and threshed as the forms of the fish darted at its body. The tank was all clouded now and scarlet splashes spread out against the glass; water and blood slopped over the edge and the cat's howls rose to a high, keening cry. Its body trembled and vibrated and I could see Mandrake's arm quiver with the effort as he held the dying beast beneath the surface, his hand just out of reach of the darting barbs of the killer piranha.

I sat back in my chair and looked steadily at Mandrake. Diane Morris stumbled over towards the cocktail bar with her hands over her ears. A bead of sweat trickled down Mandrake's face. Otto had climbed down from the divan and was retching into his handkerchief.

So no-one was really prepared for it when Charley Fong crashed through the saloon double doors with eyeballs bursting from a yellow mask which had turned to off-white. He made straight for Mandrake and his face spelt murder. What made it worse was that he had a big meat-axe in his hand.

CHAPTER EIGHT

Underwater

I

I THOUGHT it was time I contributed something to the afternoon's entertainment. I went out of my chair in a long dive, going in low under Charley Fong's guard, hoping to avoid the flailing axe. I hit the carpet with my shoulder, bounced and then caught him just below the knees. He grunted once and then we were turning and he came down on top of me with a crash. He was mighty heavy for such a small man.

I caught a glimpse of Mandrake; he hadn't moved. He still had his hand inside the top of the tank and his eyes had a fixed expression. We hit the floor with a noise like thunder. Charley Fong gave a sobbing sigh like all the breath was expelled from his lungs and the meat-axe left his hand and went skidding across the cabin. Otto had got to the Luger by now and he was coming up fast. I put my hand over Charley Fong's face and pressed him down into the carpet.

As I rolled I saw Diane Morris pass between me and Mandrake. I couldn't see what she was doing. It was Scarpini I was worried about but fortunately he didn't show. I wriggled on top just as Otto got to us with the Luger.

"Take it easy with him," I said.

Otto nodded. "Sure pal," he said in a gentle voice. He laid the gun barrel almost reflectively alongside the little Chinaman's head. He gave a choking grunt and went limp as it stroked him to sleep. I got up then and went and sat in the armchair. Otto gave a long sigh and looked around the saloon like he didn't know where to start. I picked up the meat cleaver and put it down on a table. Otto started dragging Charley Fong out. His heels left a long groove in the carpet.

I sat down in the armchair again. "Excitable staff you got," I told Mandrake. He had taken his hand away from the top of the tank. The water was black now but I could still see the corpse of the cat jumping as the fish attacked it. Bone shone white in the revolving mass. Mandrake wiped his hand on a large handkerchief he took from an inner pocket. He examined it absently but found no sign of damage.

"I suppose I ought to thank you," he said.

"For what?" I said. "Protecting my own interests?"

He smiled thinly. "You were, then, mainly motivated by the remaining 4,000 dollars?"

"I was thinking of the little fellow, too," I said. "I didn't want to see him get hurt. After all, it was his cat."

"I must say you passed my test admirably," he said, going over to the cocktail cabinet. He handed me a glass. Diane Morris sat down on the arm of a chair. Her face looked white and she bit on a handkerchief. Mandrake handed her a glass of bourbon. She drank it like it was soda water and some of the colour came back into her face.

Mandrake turned back to face me again. "It was, you might say, a clash of loyalties solved by compromise."

I shrugged. "It was only a cat," I said. "Nothing to get het up about either way."

"Your reaction was just what mine would have been in

similar circumstances," he said. "We were in no danger.
I always carry extra insurance."

He put his hand into the back of the tank vent and came
up with an efficient-looking revolver. It had the safety
catch off. He lifted his glass.

"To men of action," he said.

I lifted my glass and we drank.

2

"Thanks for the entertainment," I said. "I really ought
to be going. I'll try and get something moving tonight and
come out and see you tomorrow afternoon."

Mandrake, Diane Morris and I stood under the awning
on *The Gay Lady*'s stern deck. Otto lounged at the rail
watching us while three useful-looking sailors in blue
jerseys broke open crates they brought up from a hatchway.
I saw steel oxygen cylinders, aqua-lung equipment, even
a big, heavy rubber diving suit with a brass helmet.

"Fond of swimming?" I asked.

Mandrake made an eloquent movement of his shoulders.
"I like to come prepared for everything," he said.
"Grosvenor may have thrown something into the water.
So . . . Scarpini's a pretty good diver. He handles all that
side for me."

I looked at Diane Morris. She seemed to have recovered
her spirits but there was still a curious colour round her
eyes. "Incidentally," I said to Mandrake, "who locked me
in the deep-freeze compartment? Just for the record."

He turned blandly to Diane Morris. "Why don't you
run Mr. Faraday ashore, my dear? You're both going to
the Catamaran and Mr. Faraday will want to pick up his
car. I can get Otto to go across with the dinghy later and
bring the boat back. You look as if the trip would do you
good."

"Thanks for the information," I said. "See you to-morrow."

I went down the gangway into the boat with Diane Morris following. Mandrake didn't move. He stood by the rail looking down with inscrutable eyes. I watched him till *The Gay Lady* dwindled in the distance.

3

Diane Morris set the boat out across the choppy water of the harbour with the skill of an expert. She sat in the stern handling the tiller like Long John Silver and evaded my eyes.

"I expect you think badly of me," she said after a bit.

"Does it matter what I think?" I said. "This is a pretty tough racket you're in, that's for sure."

She looked at me with anger smouldering on her face. "If it weren't for Mandrake I shouldn't be mixed up in this."

"I thought he was your boyfriend," I said.

She laughed. It was an ugly sound, chopped off by the noise of the motor. "He's a beast," she said. "I hate him. You saw what he did to that cat."

"Then why work for him?" I said.

She shrugged. "Necessity. He picked up some of my brother's gambling checks back in Chicago. I'm paying off the debt."

I was silent for a moment.

"I see. So you're not really a hundred per cent for their side?"

"All I want is out," she said angrily. "They're like a pack of wolves aboard there, with Mandrake sitting in the middle enjoying it all. He's a sadist; and he won't stop coming after me. He's got some crazy idea I should marry him."

I said nothing. We were running into the jetty before she spoke again.

" You look a square guy," she said. " Perhaps we could help one another."

" I'll think about it," I said. " How do I know I can trust you?"

" You don't," she said. But she said it in a special way and I could see no double-talk in her eyes. I decided to buy, but at the same time to give nothing away.

" Who put the finger on Grosvenor?" I said.

" His name's Melissa," she replied.

I let that go.

" Otto and Scarpini, of course," she said.

" The same guys that shut me in the ice-box," I said.

She nodded. That brought me to something else.

" You think Charley Fong will be all right?" I asked. " I rather liked the little guy. He's got guts and I gather he's not too keen on Mandrake either."

She smiled then and shook her head. " I don't think he's in any danger. Like Mandrake said, it was his cat."

She throttled back the engine and we nosed gently into the jetty. I tied up the painter while she switched off and we went up the steps. I could see the shambling figure of the Ancient Mariner making with tottering excitement towards us. I grabbed Diane's arm, turned her smartly about and led her back to the blue sedan. We got in; the heat off the cushions was stifling. I wound down the windows while she started up. She reversed back along the jetty and round the right-angle, made a three-point turn and then gunned along past the Police Office. The Ancient opened his mouth and made like he had something to tell me, then clammed up as if he had thought better of it. He turned on his heel and walked away down towards the boat hire quay.

" Drive round town for a bit," I told Diane Morris. " We haven't finished yet."

She went on to the edge of town and took a smoothly tarmaced road that went round in a curve along the bay; the white sand had the pinkish tinge caused by thousands of crushed conch shells.

"What do you know about Mandrake?" I asked her.

"It's not his real name," she said. She named his name. It meant nothing to me.

"He's a Chicago big shot," she said. "In all the rackets there, from gambling, slot machines and cat-houses to the numbers racket. He also has a legit meat-packing business that acts as a front for the rest."

"He would," I said. I lit two cigarettes from my pack, took one out of my mouth and gave it to her. She dragged on it gratefully.

"Where does this character Lloyd come in?" I asked.

"That's another legit angle," she said. "He's in insurance. Prints his own money. One of the Chicago Lloyds. Everything above board there. Mandrake is in with everybody. Lloyd just lends him the boat whenever he asks for it. It covers up a lot of things."

"It figures," I said. "You still haven't told me much about yourself."

She stopped the car and we sat looking out across the wide curve of the bay to the palms on the opposite shore. There were only about five people on the whole sweep of the cape and about two more in the water. A half dozen cars were parked on the concrete esplanade farther down. It was pretty crowded for this part of the world.

"Not much to tell," she said after a long silence. "Night club hostess most of the time. No better than I ought to be."

She leaned forward suddenly and kissed me full on the lips. I didn't do much to resist. The kiss lasted for about half an hour and when I finally opened my eyes I figured it must be around sunset. I was surprised to find it was still light.

"What was that for?" I said.

She laughed and adjusted her complexion in the car mirror. "Bonus," she said.

"On top of the 5,000," I said. "I must be dreaming. You underestimate yourself. You're much better than anyone has a right to be."

She laughed again and started the motor.

"By the way," I said as we drove back to pick up my car, "though it might be said we're working together, no more sleep-walking from now on. I did come on holiday with my secretary and she's rather jealous."

"Lucky her," she said with a grin. "But I reserve the right to break the amnesty if the occasion presents itself."

I let that go. She dropped me off at the jetty, waved and gunned off. Mandrake had given me back my keys so I went on over to the Caddy. I didn't go near the Police Office. I just got in the big car, finished my cigarette and then sneaked on out of town.

4

Stella was lying on her tummy sunning herself on the marble patio by the big swim-pool at the Catamaran. She was still wearing the white-two-piece and she made Cleopatra look like a two-bit deodorant advertisement. It seemed like a hundred years since I had last seen her. I smacked her hard where it would do most good.

"Mike!" She went up in the air. One or two people round the edge of the pool turned and looked curiously at us. I saw the fat guy with the Frankfurter sausage fingers staring. I thought he looked jealous.

"How did you know it was me?" I asked.

Stella looked at me over the top of her dark glasses. "Nobody else has got that loathsomely familiar touch," she said.

" Thanks," I said. " You're in a flattering mood this afternoon."

She took off the glasses and smiled. She looked great when she smiled. In fact I had to turn back to the waters of the pool to stop myself from being dazzled.

Then her face was warm against mine and white teeth nipped my ear. " You're just a big softie, really," she said and went off the edge of the pool in a shallow dive. I didn't have time to work that one out before the spray came drenching down over me. She grinned, thrashed around the pool a couple of times and came on out. Globules of water shone like crystals on the very fine down which covered the brown firmness of her thighs. I was always uncomfortably aware of her in a manner very different to that of girls like Diane Morris.

I got up suddenly and she smiled again. She put her arm in mine and we took a turn around the pool. In between gazing in her eyes and the occasional arm squeeze, I filled her in on Mandrake and the yacht and the day's developments. She didn't say much. For all you could have told we were just a couple of honeymooners. We had the old fat guy fooled anyway; he still gave me sour looks mingled with envy every time we passed him.

" So?" said Stella as we stopped by her canework chair again.

" So I'd like you to keep an eye on Diane Morris and act as a liason between me and Clay," I said.

She nodded. " Will do."

" Look," I said. " I'm really sorry about the holiday. I'll make it up to you. And anyways, the way things are going, we may have it wrapped up in another twenty-four hours."

" Forget it," she said. " Only thing worries me is the Morris girl. I don't like the idea of you working together."

" That's exactly what she said," I told her.

She looked nonplussed. I laid my hand on her shoulder.

" Forget her," I advised Stella. " You've never had any competition and you know it."

" It must be the balmy air and the sunshine," said Stella drily. " Another week of this and you'll be getting positively sentimental."

" Sorry," I said. " I won't let it happen again."

We went on into the hotel.

5

I went on up to my room, had a shower and lay on the bed for a few minutes. It was now around six. I pulled the phone over towards me and called Clay. He was still at the office. He sounded worried.

" Sorry about the date," I said. " I got invited out to take tea on the yacht instead."

" We saw something of that," he said. " Ian spotted you with the binoculars. He wanted us to go out and rescue you at one time."

" Good job it never came to that," I said. I filled him in on the whole set-up.

" Very nice," he said. " We're still a long way from proof but it fills in a few useful gaps in our knowledge."

" Anything your end?" I asked.

" Nothing on the positive side," he said grimly. " We got the coloured boy from the Cucumber Cay freeze plant."

" Good work," I said.

" Unfortunately not," said Colonel Clay stiffly. " His body was washed up about five miles along the coast this morning. Doc Griffith says there are no marks of violence. Death by drowning."

" Convenient," I said.

" What's your next move?" said the Colonel.

" If you agree I'd like to have a crack at the yacht tonight," I said. " What I'll be looking for is evidence to link Mandrake and his chums with Melissa. There must be some Mafia records aboard; names or details of money transactions."

There was a long silence at the other end of the phone. I could almost hear the wheels going around in Clay's head.

" Do you think this is wise?" he said at last. " We can give you very little official coverage on such on operation."

" I'm not asking for that," I said. " And wisdom has never been my strong point. You asked me to string along on this job and now it's become a personal thing between me and Mandrake. After all he is from the States and I've had a long experience in dealing with his kind. What you could do is keep a look-out with night-glasses and if you see the boat on fire or something on that scale, come on out."

He chuckled. " All right, we'll play. But what if the yacht up-anchors? We lifted the shipping restrictions this afternoon."

I thought hard. " I'll fix it so you'll know where we're going," I said. " Could you get Phillips to do me a duplicate of the map-tracing Melissa left? Only with the bearings a bit scrambled—just enough to land him up about ten miles from the target."

I could almost hear Colonel Clay smiling on his end of the phone.

" Excellent, Michael," he said at last. " I'll get Ian on to that right away. How shall we get it to you?"

" I'll be going out about ten tonight," I said. " It'll be no good until after dark. I'll ask Stella to pick it up at your house tonight around nine. The map will give me a good bargaining card with Mandrake if I'm caught. I must look as if I'm earning my thousand dollars."

" I'm glad you got something out of this business," he said.

" I'll get Ian to make that a true reference so we can

keep tabs on *The Gay Lady*. Anything else you want us to do?"

" I don't think so," I said. " So long as you're standing by tonight."

He gave me his home address. I took it down and we said good night. I went out on to the balcony. The pool was almost empty now. One or two couples were still swimming out in the sea but the majority of the guests looked like they were resting up for dinner. I didn't see Diane Morris.

I went back to the phone and dialled Stella's room. I told her what I'd arranged with Clay and she said she'd be at his house dead on nine so she could be back at the Catamaran by nine-thirty. This would give me ample time for what I wanted to do. I asked her to get the Caddy's tank filled with gas just in case I needed to give it a lot of use that night. I told her I would leave the keys at the hotel desk. Then I lay back on the bed and stared at the ceiling. After a little while I dozed.

6

It was almost dark. I lay in the comfortable dusk of the hotel room and feathered smoke through my nostrils. I looked at the dial of my wrist-watch. The hands stood at a minute or two after nine-thirty. The time wasn't all that critical, as I had all night, but if I left it too late the people on the yacht might turn in which would make it difficult. I would like to arrive on board some time between eleven and midnight when the odds were that they would be drinking in the saloon or ashore.

Trouble was I didn't know how long it would take me to make it out to the yacht with the gear I'd have with me and then I had to find a suitable jumping-off point and stash the car. I stubbed out my cigarette in the ash-tray by the bed and listened to the breeze and the sound of the surf.

Five more minutes passed and then I heard the hum of a car coming up the road outside the hotel; the light of the headlamps sliced across the balcony. The motor stopped and the door slammed; high heels beat a tattoo across the patio. I got up then, shut the balcony door and switched on the light. I put on the jacket of my lightweight suit and adjusted my tie in the mirror. I was just doing up a waterproof bundle when there came a tap on the door. It was Stella.

" All set ?" she asked.

I nodded. " How's things with Colonel Clay ?"

She smiled. " As gallant as ever."

She handed me a slip of paper. As far as I could see Phillips had done a good job on the tracing. I crumpled it a few times to make it look like Melissa had carried it in his pocket for a while.

" Colonel Clay sent this too," said Stella. She handed me an envelope. Inside it was a set of bearings.

" That's the real position," she went on. " The Colonel thought you might care to memorise it in case things got really difficult. Then if the yacht isn't at the fake position they'll know where to go. Colonel Clay called it the final bargaining counter."

" That's his military mind," I said.

Stella caught at my arm. Her eyes were wide and worried. " Mike, you will be careful won't you ?"

" Don't worry, sweetie," I said. I kissed her lightly. " You know me."

" That's the worry," said Stella.

We went out. I locked the door and took the car keys back from her. I patted her arm as I went by.

" Clay will keep you in touch," I said.

She stood and looked after me as I went on down the corridor and down the stairs. I went out to the Caddy and checked the tank. Stella had used only a gallon and the needle read just under the full. There was a bright moon so I used only the sidelights. I put the waterproof package on the back seat. I went out of the car park as quietly as I could and on down the dusty road that led to Stanley Bay. A few days ago I had used it only once. Now I went up and down it so many times I was beginning to feel like a commuter.

There was still a luminous glow on the sea and any other night I should have thought the scene pretty beautiful, as I threaded one bay and headland after another. But all I could remember was that Mandrake and his trigger boys had pretty sharp eyes, whatever they lacked in marbles, and the moon was a deal too bright for my taste when swimming out. That was why I had brought the package.

There was no other traffic on the road at that time of night; it was only a few minutes after ten when I hit Stanley Bay. It was a bit more animated at night time and neon-lit bars and clubs made a red and green glow in the sky over the little town. I tooled the car on down to thread the rear of the jetties where the Police and Harbour Master's offices were and came out near the spot where I had sat with Diane earlier that afternoon.

I parked the Caddy in rear of a big set of stone bollards where it wouldn't be too conspicuous. Nothing moved on the beach but from far off there came the monotonous blare of a dance band and the rhythmic shuffle of dancers' feet. I took out the car keys and put them in my pocket and buttoned up the waterproof cover over the car. I didn't know how long I was going to be away and the heap was on hire after all.

I took the waterproof bundle and walking on the balls of my feet I high-tailed it in as casual a manner as possible down to the back of the concrete esplanade. Towards the edge of the harbour the buildings thinned out and there was a jumble of rocky outcrops and stone fortifications dating from the days when Stanley Bay was an outpost of Britain's Colonial empire. The noise of the sea came up loud and the water slapped at the stones and undersides of the moored boats with a sound that would have put the nerves of a sensitive man on edge.

But I'm not a sensitive man and to me it sounded just like water slapping on the underside of stonework and boat bottoms. What I had to be on guard against was fishermen and the odd longshore loafer like the Ancient Mariner. I also had to make sure I didn't give myself too far to swim.

The Gay Lady, visible only by the light along the length of her ports and her masthead riding lights was about half a mile out from shore anyway and I didn't aim to turn the swim into a marathon.

Of course, underwater swimming at night wasn't exactly unknown in these parts but I didn't want any frightened fishermen ringing up the Police Office—or anyone else. I found a spot that seemed suitable and stripped off my clothes behind a big stone breakwater. Then I stashed them under the base of the wall and piled as many stones on them as I could find. I had already emptied my pockets of money and anything else of value before I came out. Being lightweight, they made only a small compact bundle. I was already wearing swimming trunks underneath my clothes.

Out of the kit I carried I took a waterproof body belt which fastened round my waist with webbing straps. Into this I put my wrist watch, a small compass and the piece of paper with the fake map stencilled on it. I had already memorised the bearings on the other sheet. I carried a knife in a rubberised sheath which was slung from the body belt. I put on the frogman flippers I had brought from the hotel, the glass goggles and clamped the mouthpiece with the rubber tubing firmly between my teeth.

I tested the ping-pong ball arrangement in its cage at the end of the tube. It was a simple kit such as youngsters use at the seaside but nothing more elaborate was needed here. I was a slow swimmer, like I said, but I had trained myself to swim a few feet beneath the surface of the water and the tip of the tubing when I came up to take air wouldn't notice with the shimmer on the water. At least that was the idea. But I put my faith in the rest of the gear I carried, more than anything else. I had wrapped the waterproof covering round this and carried it in one hand as I swam. It was a powerful underwater harpoon gun used for spearing fish.

It had a nasty-looking harpoon in the barrel and the whole gadget worked off compressed air. Round the light alloy handle I had secured a length of thick twine. Better still, the harmless end of the gun contained a small glass dome in a thick rubber mounting. This was a waterproof electric torch which worked off a subsidiary grip on the handle. There wasn't much else I could do and the whole enterprise was a bit shaky but there wasn't any point in hanging around to see the dawn come up, so I took a mental note where *The Gay Lady* was, tip-toed elegantly into the water and let myself sink slowly down behind the nearest boats.

I waited until the water reached my chin; it was damn cold at first. Then I took a breath, adjusted my nose-clip and went down under the surface. I started to swim out towards the yacht.

7

The tide was setting out of the harbour which helped things considerably; I settled down about three feet beneath the surface and more or less let the current take me out. It would be a different story coming back but I could tackle that when the time came. I kicked gently with my legs to avoid leaving a wash and tooled quietly along beneath the water, taking a rough guide from the riding lights of the nearest sizeable yacht to me, which was on a line with *The Gay Lady*.

I wanted to hit Mandrake's boat on the shady side, away from the lit gangway that faced out to sea. At any rate I could count on the tide taking me straight out with minimum effort on my part until I reached the hull. Every now and then I eased up a foot or so to replenish the air in the tube before coming down to the lower level. I had hit my stride by now and was making easy breast-strokes and the water felt warmer. When I judged I was safely past the first yacht I risked surfacing for a few seconds in the blackness beyond.

The lights of *The Gay Lady* burned nearer and clearer and she seemed a lot higher out of the water. I could hear the dance band pounding from the shore; it carried a long way in the still night air. Out here it was very quiet except for the minute slapping noise made by the wavelets. I went under again abruptly as a beam of light chopped the water ahead of me. A rain of potato peelings, used packages and other garbage hit the water. I heard the clink of a metal pail just before I went below and then someone closed the cabin hatch.

I couldn't see much underneath the surface but I dove a little deeper and soon spotted the hulls of more moored craft which I hadn't seen earlier. Another minute or two and I should have run into them on the course I was making. I trod water as soon as I was past and when I came up for a second time I could see that I was a long way from the shore. Chains of lights burned in the mauve dusk of the bay and were re-echoed round the headland.

I faced to my front again and saw *The Gay Lady* almost as far off as ever but now more to the left on the seaward side. It was evident that what current there was was setting me in to the rocks and the wall on the other side of the harbour. I worked round with hardly a ripple in the water and set off swimming strongly more to the left in order to

compensate for the drift. I gauged I had been in the sea
upwards of half an hour already; it was farther than I
figured. That or else I wasn't the swimmer I thought I
was.

I went under again, guiding myself this time by *The
Gay Lady*'s masthead light which was riding around in a
gentle arc. This way I had something constant to aim for
and I was able to allow for the westward flow of the water
out here. After ten minutes I surfaced again and made out
a largish buoy bobbing about between me and the yacht.
It was only a few hundred yards now so I hung gratefully
on to a metal ring on the buoy and got my breath and eased
my aching muscles.

The final stretch was a lot easier. The water was dark and
there were only a few bow ports alight on my side, evidently
from the crew's quarters, and these were curtained. I risked
the last hundred yards on the surface, as I wanted to pick
my spot for boarding with care. No sound came from the
yacht and there didn't seem to be anyone on deck. I took
off the nose-clip and eased the rubber mounting out of my
mouth and breathed real air again.

I hit the hull of *The Gay Lady* with the lightest of bumps
and trod water, pushing myself along the hull while I
looked for a way up. She seemed like the Queen Mary
from this low down. I transferred the mouthpiece and tubing
to the hand carrying the spear-gun and then I caught hold
of the rubbing-strake. I clung there until I got my bearings
and made my way hand over hand, taking care not to
scratch the hull with my gear, before I found the nearside
gangway. It wasn't properly down and I didn't want to
use it anyway, but there was a zinc chain hanging into the
water.

I eased out my piece of twine and eventually tied the
whole bundle—fish-harpoon, face-piece and flippers to the
chain. I had put everything in the waterproof wrapping
and tied it with a knot I could undo in a hurry if I had

E

to. Then I eased a little way along the hull, seized the rubbing-strake and hauled myself up out of the water until my right hand could get hold of a deck stanchion. By now I had got my left foot on to the rubbing-strake and lifted slowly up to deck level. I shot a quick glance around but there was nobody in sight, so I insinuated myself over the rail and on to the deck.

I loosened the knife in its sheath, made sure I knew where I'd come aboard and started to prowl along the companion way towards the bows. I wanted to see what the crew was doing first before I decided on the next move. Keeping in the shadow I pussy-footed up to the forward cabin entrance; there was a big hatch on deck. I couldn't see anything but I could hear at least two men talking and a radio playing softly. That disposed of half the crew; so far as I knew Mandrake had three deck-hands and a paid hire-skipper, but what part they played in the set-up I didn't know. I had to treat them as enemy and act accordingly.

I made it quietly back to mid-ships. I gave the main saloon a miss and tried the door through which we'd gone when we first came abroad. There had been doors leading off this corridor before we got to the saloon and it seemed the most obvious start. I slid the hatch back and lifted my feet cautiously over the sill. There was the same companion way with dim night-lights burning; the same smell of diesel oil and salt and, far off, the faint throbbing of a generator. I risked leaving the door an inch or two ajar in case I had to exit in a hurry and walking on tip-toe tried the first opening I came to. It swung outwards on the corridor and no light showed underneath.

I hesitated only a moment and then stepped over the sill, shut the door behind me, locked it with the key which was in it and snapped on the brass light switch I found on my right hand. The door was made of teak a good inch thick and would take some time to break down. There was a wooden bookshelf with navigation volumes and the latest novels; a model sailing ship in a bottle; a fake marble wash basin with chrome fittings set in a mahogany alcove, a long mirror set over the basin. There was a big wooden bunk on one side of the cabin with a candlewick bedspread on it. It hadn't been slept in.

Set under two portholes at present covered coyly with minute chintz curtains was a big, solid table screwed to the deck. It had a glass top and the surface was strewn with maps and navigation instruments. I went over to the bunk; there was another shelf alongside it, braced into the angle of two walls. On the shelf was a leather mounted photo frame. It contained a studio portrait full-length of a rather handsome man with light curly hair; he was in his mid-forties I should have said and wore a blue uniform with brass buttons.

I made a moué in the mirror, figured I had gotten into the skipper's cabin, said " Sorry, chum," and doused the light preparatory to getting the hell out. I had just turned the key in the lock and was starting to ease open the door when I heard footsteps in the corridor. I risked leaving it open about half an inch and glued my eye to the crack. One of the seamen passed within two feet of me; he had his head down and was humming " Home Sweet Home " tunelessly to himself under his breath.

He went on down the corridor to the crew's quarters. That made three; all accounted for except the skipper. I might expect him to be on shore or basking in the limelight of Mandrake's personality in the saloon. Unless Mandrake had gone ashore as well. I opened my waist-belt and sneaked a glance at my watch. It was already 11.40 and I had to get moving if I didn't want to be surprised.

Farther down the corridor, past the big sliding doors that I knew led to the saloon was another teak door; I made it in three seconds flat, stepping on the balls of my feet, my heart working in time to the muffled thud of the dynamo.

If the skipper would have the best accommodation after the owner, it seemed reasonable that they would both be somewhere around the same part of the ship. I hit the jackpot as soon as I got inside. It wasn't a cabin but a suite of three rooms; study, bedroom and dressing room with an adjoining bathroom and shower. It was furnished in the same style as the saloon—that is to say pretty luxurious —but I had no eye for the décor.

I locked the main entrance just as soon as I had made sure the place was empty; I didn't waste time on the rest but went straight for the room set aside as a study. There was a big desk in there, with ornate brass fittings and a green leather inlaid top that wouldn't have looked out of place in the Louvre. I bet it came from there at that.

The keys being in the desk ought to have warned me. I tried three drawers, opening them with keys on the bunch I found dangling from the top one. I riffed through a lot of stuff without finding anything of interest. I had already been in here five minutes and I couldn't risk much longer. Then I found what I was looking for. It was a little blue book, only about the size of a pocket diary. It was full of names and amounts of money, but it looked as beautiful as the score of Beethoven's Choral Symphony to me. The name of Melissa occurred several times and there was Mandrake also, only in his real name.

There was a lot more at the back of the book but I could leave that until I could chew the fat with Colonel Clay. There were addresses too; in fact what seemed like the whole set-up of the Chicago branch of the Mafia. I put the book in my body-belt, clipped the waterproof pouch closed, put everything back as I had found it and then re-locked the desk, leaving the keys hanging from the top drawer.

I took the knife out of my belt, tip-toed out to the main bedroom, tripping the light switches after me. I had dried off long ago in this warm air, so I didn't leave any wet hoof-marks on Mandrake's expensive carpets. Perhaps I was a bit careless or maybe things had gone too well. Whatever it was, I got outside the door, turned back along the deck and bumped into a shape which had just come through the sliding doors from the big saloon.

He gave a yell like I had already stuck him with the knife and slammed up against me with his fists flailing; one of them caught me in the mouth and put me off balance. I fell back against a metal vent and the knife bounced from my hand. Scarpini kept on yelling and kept on coming; I caught him a hard one against the side of the face with my balled fist and he went down in a heap.

I leaped over him as someone blundered through the saloon doors sending light scorching over the corridor; by this time the whole ship was roused. I made the English guy Bannister look like the tortoise in the fable by putting distance between myself and the guys in the corridor. Lights were going on everywhere; there were shouts from the crew and the thud of feet on deck. I heard Scarpini yell something again as I crashed back the sliding door to the open air. I could see one of the seamen tumbling out of the fore hatch and there were more heavy feet behind me.

I mentally noted where I had come over the side, made for it as close as I could. I vaulted over the rail far from cleanly, caught my leg a numbing blow on a wire somewhere, and then made it into the haven of dark water.

8

Through the broken, heaving surface of the water I could see blinding lights. I sidled away into the darkness of the yacht hull and made for the companion way. Someone on deck had switched on the big arc-lights they used for loading and unloading. That would be Mandrake. This was a bit more than I had figured on. My lungs were bursting from my enforced sprint and I would have to come up in a very short time without the underwater outfit. Somehow I couldn't see these boys figuring I had been drowned— if they had recognised me, that is. Or were they expecting me?

The probing pencil of a searchlight reached across the water. I felt I could hear faint shouting. My best chance was to stay on the landward side of *The Gay Lady* and hope that the lights and the commotion would attract some attention. I hoped Clay would restrain Phillips' enthusiasm; I didn't want them blundering out now even though I could have done with some help. Going off half-cock on a thing like this could be more hindrance than otherwise.

Evidently Mandrake thought so too because the searchlight went out soon after and the shouting died away. I risked coming up then and took a gulp of air under the sheer of the yacht's hull. All the area round my side of the ship was as bright as a Fourth of July carnival. I dived again and came up only a few yards from the gangway. I swam underwater and had just got close enough to grab it when it came down with a rumble of chains. I went down with it and found my bundle still fixed on with the twine. I came up directly underneath the platform and took another gulp of air. Then something split the darkness, silvered the sea-surface with brief foam and disappeared.

I got under the water again and saw a form in swimming trunks streaking downwards about a dozen yards away; bubbles danced towards the surface. Those damned lamps gave a good light for quite a long way underneath and it was only a question of time before I was spotted. It was Scarpini; he was more muscular than I gave him credit for with his clothes on and I saw why Mandrake had chosen him for the underwater stuff.

He was a beautiful swimmer and he turned like a grey-hound in the light of the lamps. He had my knife in one hand too which was unfortunate. He went up to breathe after a bit and I crowded in against the hull and went down to give my bundle the once-over. When I came up again Scarpini was swimming to and fro only a few yards away. It might have been beautiful except that I was in no mood for the Palm Springs water ballet. He was no Esther Williams come to that. He soon got tired of swimming around and went up for air.

I took another couple of gulps in the shadow of the hull. When he dived the next time he was a lot closer; he trod water and I could see the hair on his head streaming out like he was in a high wind. It was around then that he spotted me and he came swimming in to the attack in a fast crawl, the knife held out in his left hand away from his body and off to one side. I had seen this before. This was the most dangerous style of underwater fighting.

I kicked back behind the trailing companion way chain. The refraction of the water and the shifting lights from the surface made it difficult, but I caught his hand a glancing blow and deflected the knife. While he was off balance I grabbed the chain and kicked him as hard as I could in the stomach. He doubled up, but apart from that he didn't seem greatly affected. I danced closer to him and then he straightened up like a jack-knife and closed with me. But I had his weapon hand then.

His skin was slippery and I had difficulty in keeping my hold. His eyes looked right into mine and I felt his sharp fingers hooking into each side of my neck, looking for the jugular. I slipped away from him and kneed him in the groin. That hurt but he still didn't let go the knife.

As he released his grip I shot up and grabbed a lungful of air; I met him going down and stamped at his head but he swerved aside. I was too far from the companion way now so I waited and grabbed his arm again when he swam down. I misjudged this time and carried on past him; he lunged with the knife and I felt a numbing blow on my shoulder. Blood spiralled slowly up to the surface. I turned quickly, found I could still use my right arm and concluded it had been a superficial flesh wound.

I went limp in the water, creased up my face as though in pain; it was an old wrestler's trick but anything in the book was good enough for this situation. Scarpini turned under me and came up with the knife for a death blow. But this time I was ready for him. We were back under the hull of the boat now, driven in by the outgoing current. I came up while he was still thinking about his move.

My right hand caught his left and smashed the knife and his balled knuckles against the copper sheathing along the bottom of the ship; there were razor-edged crustaceans where the copper met the wooden planking and it split his hand through to the bone. I saw the knife weave downwards through the light beams and then I brought my knee up into the pit of his stomach. He sort of hung there for a moment and then floated up to the surface.

I went down below then and made my preparations. After my next breather I saw him reappear. He came down again, more cautiously this time but with an even bigger knife in his hand. I had to give him credit for guts though. It was then that I got to the harpoon-gun. I had tied it earlier with just one slip knot round the hollow metal stock. I loosed it now and brought it up into the firing position.

He paddled down towards me quite casually as though on an afternoon sponge-fishing expedition. He had the knife held out in his right hand this time, his crushed left making stroking motions in the water. I was right up under the yacht hull in the shadow cast by the companion way platform and he didn't see the gun until it was too late. He was only about three feet away and the light was making undulating patterns on his throat and neck.

I hoped the refraction of the water wouldn't make me miss my aim and shot him neatly through the throat; the gun made a loud hiss and bubbles shot to the surface. Scarpini turned a somersault and his body shuddered like a hooked fish. His mouth was open and his eyeballs straining from his head. He was coughing red; there were red streamers going to the surface. That and bubbles of air where the steel-bladed harpoon stuck out a foot the other side of his neck. I had taken the most powerful gun the Catamaran had to offer.

I let it drop to the floor of the harbour. I steadied myself on the metal chain and watched as Scarpini started to sink towards the bottom. He looked at me quite reflectively as he went by. I surfaced again, blinded by light and panting from exhaustion. There was a boat on the surface with two crew members in it. I noticed that without interest. The sea kept going up and down more violently than I had remembered.

My arm hurt then and I saw crimson running down among the beads of water. I felt I didn't want to die that evening. I got hold of a stanchion and slowly, like a very old man, I heaved myself aboard again. Then, after what seemed like a couple of hours, I started to walk back up on to the deck of *The Gay Lady*. Otto stood at the head of the companion way and watched me come.

CHAPTER NINE

Otto Gets Rough

I

OTTO SAT on the end of the divan and pointed his Luger at me. The gun was on my belly and I realised I was only a short trip away from Doc Griffith's dissecting table. I sat in one of Mandrake's chairs dripping sea water on his carpet and trying to look as if I knew all the answers. Diane Morris tore up another handkerchief to bind round my shoulder.

Her face looked grey.

Mr. Mandrake sat opposite the saloon from me. His pink starfish hands were folded across his stomach. He looked as calm as though he were presiding at a board meeting of his frozen meat company.

" What happened to Scarpini ? " he said.

" He had an accident," I said. " He cut himself on a fish hook."

" That was careless of him," said Mandrake gently. He didn't change expression. His eyes focussed on the tall glass on the table in front of him.

" This means a switch in plans. He was quite my best diver. Otto here doesn't even know how to swim."

There was no difference of tone but Otto turned white around the mouth. Mandrake looked back at me again.

" I trust this doesn't mean a change of sides, Mr. Faraday? I'm sure you have a satisfactory explanation."

I took the hard way out. " I just quit," I said heavily. " I'll send on the thousand dollars."

He put up one of the pink starfish and waved it gently. " It isn't as easy as all that, Mr. Faraday. People are not in the habit of quitting my service until I've finished with them. And I'll decide when."

His eyes fixed unwaveringly on mine. A long sliver of pain tore through my shoulder as Diane Morris tightened up the bandage. I winced. Otto chuckled to himself. He didn't take the gun off my belly.

" What did you come aboard for, Mr. Faraday?" asked Mandrake, still in that soft dreamy tone. He sat and looked at the ceiling of the saloon as though he had all the time in the world. I fixed my gaze on Mr. Mandrake's hands and tried to ignore Otto's gun barrel. I wasn't very successful.

" I was afraid you might sail before I reported the good news," I said.

" We shall see," he said gently. " Did you search him?" he asked Otto.

The big man looked taken aback. " He ain't wearin' no more than a glorified G-string," he said warily.

Mr. Mandrake silenced him. " Idiot," he said in a tone which crackled contempt. " Do it now."

Otto withered up. He got to his feet. He put the gun in his pocket. That didn't make any difference. There was a seaman, the one who had passed me in the corridor, standing just at the back of the settee. He had broken teeth, an unshaven face and a mean eye. He wore a dark blue jersey with *Gay Lady* stitched across the front of it in white piping. That was the only gay thing about him. He had a loaded shotgun held across his chest, which was more important still, and he looked like he knew how to use it. He didn't say anything. He didn't need to with that kind of artillery.

Otto came over and fished in the empty sheath which had contained my knife. He found nothing. Diane Morris finished adjusting the bandage round my shoulder and stood away. She put a drink in my hand. Otto fumbled around some more. He turned to Mandrake, half-shrugged. Mr. Mandrake turned his eyes up to the ceiling again.

" The belt, fool," he said patiently.

Otto searched the belt. He brought out the small items, including the compass. He missed the map reference because I'd folded it small and pushed it up into the stitching inside the lining. I figured he'd have missed a rhino with his big fingers and that technique. But even he could hardly miss the last item in the belt. He brought out Mandrake's blue notebook and laid it down on the table in front of him. Then he went and sat down on the divan and got out the Luger again.

Mr. Mandrake said nothing. He poked at the notebook with one of the pink starfish and turned it over curiously. He didn't seem surprised. The air in the saloon suddenly seemed to have turned hot and thundery.

" You were saying something about good news just now, Mr. Faraday," he said. " I may say that you could do with some after this." It was almost time to play my top card but I decided to hang on to the last minute. I sipped at my drink. It seemed to be composed of ninety-nine per cent bourbon. My silence seemed to madden Otto but Mandrake didn't change expression.

" We have means of persuasion if you persist in this unco-operative attitude, Mr. Faraday," he said amiably. He shrugged his blunt shoulders.

" Oh, don't think for one moment I was referring to you. I can see that you are made of durable stuff. Your reputation has preceded you. And your name is not unknown in Chicago. What I had in mind was something a little more entertaining. The lady is beginning to outlive her usefulness. Before we contacted you her utility was marginal, but now . . ."

He let out the air in his mouth with a soft noise. It was pretty expressive. He glanced at Diane Morris, gave her a brief smile then looked back at me.

" Are you familiar with the practices of the Chinese river pirates, Mr. Faraday? I have made quite a study of such out-of-the-way things. They are still very much an active force, even under the Communists."

" So?" I said.

" So this, Mr. Faraday. They have very unpleasant habits. One of them concerns the treatment of their prisoners of war. They tie their victim to the prow of one of their war junks and incise his stomach. They then cut the intestine and attach it to a large cork float. When the tide goes out, the gut floats away, yard after yard. They say it reduces even the strongest men to tears."

" Sounds like some fun," I said. " I didn't know they were that ingenious around Chicago."

I didn't look at Diane Morris's face. Sweat trickled down Otto's. It was so quiet in the saloon that I could hear the whine of the generator right at the other end of the boat. A fly landed on one of Mr. Mandrake's hands. He didn't move. After a moment it flew away.

" Think it over, Mr. Faraday," he said smoothly. " I'm sure you have more regard for the girl. Even a soldier of fortune like yourself must draw the line somewhere."

He had me there. I finished up my drink, put the empty glass down on the carpet at my feet.

" All right," I said, " you can cut the melodrama. I think we can do a deal. I got a map tracing showing where the loot is stashed."

Otto smiled, the seaman at the back of the divan lowered the shotgun and leaned it against the cabin wall. The temperature went down.

For the first time Mr. Mandrake reached out for his drink.

" Excellent, Mr. Faraday, excellent. I was sure I could rely on your sound commonsense. Now let's get down to business. And remember, it's your lives you are playing with, so choose your words carefully."

" I've got the map here," I said. I fished in the body belt and brought out the tracing. Mandrake turned up his eyes to the ceiling again as though asking God to witness Otto's incompetence and the big man turned pink to the roots of his hair. He started to mumble something but the look on Mandrake's face stopped the words in his throat.

I passed over the tracing. " It's my guess it's under water," I said.

He spread out the piece of paper on the table in front of him and examined it intently. One pink hand smoothed out the crumples in it.

" I'm not very hot on navigation but I'd bet it's not far from this island," I went on. " Grosvenor wouldn't have risked hiding whatever was bothering him where anyone could find it easily. So I figure he's left a clue to the loot in a water-proof box or something on the bottom somewhere."

Mandrake nodded. " A reasonable assumption." He lifted his head. " Where did you get this, Mr. Faraday? I should hate to think that this material had reached me through the courtesy of the Stanley Bay Police H.Q."

" They won't be there, if that's what you're thinking," I said. " I found the tracing in Grosvenor's room. It was screwed up small and stuffed in a crack in a drawer of his dressing table, in a spot where nobody would have thought of looking."

" Except for you," he said. " A remarkable coincidence."

" Use your marbles," I told him. " The local police boys are amateurs at this sort of game. Lost dogs are more in their line. I'm a trained operator. In L.A. we got characters who'd sew a dollar bill into their navel lining if it showed a profit. I have to keep a jump ahead of them to go on eating every week."

Otto grinned. Even the corners of Mr. Mandrake's mouth relaxed a little.

" Very well, Mr. Faraday, I'll buy it. I'll leave the matter of this book for the moment. But we'll go into it later." He stood up. " At the moment I'm in need of a diver. You will be that diver, Mr. Faraday. That is if you place any value on your own survival. You might even earn your remaining 4,000 dollars."

He handed his glass to Diane Morris. " I need another drink, my dear. And you look as though you need one yourself. A re-fill, Mr. Faraday?"

I took the glass Diane gave me. She didn't look directly at me. Mandrake handed the map tracing to Otto.

" Give this to the Captain and tell him to work out the position. We sail within the next hour."

He turned back to me and Diane. He laughed shortly.

" We are going on a treasure hunt, Mr. Faraday. Here's to success."

2

The Gay Lady throbbed gently as she rose to the swell, her engines throttled back, driving her smoothly through the water. The lights of Stanley Bay Harbour receded in the middle distance as we turned to set course in the open sea. I sat in a corner of the wheelhouse wearing a borrowed seaman's sweater and a pair of blue trousers. I clutched a mug of hot coffee and thought out my next move. Diane Morris sat tensed up on a leather swivel chair opposite me. Nobody in particular watched me. They didn't need to.

The ugly-looking seaman who'd held the shotgun stood at the wheel now and steered the yacht; he looked just as much at home. He didn't look at me; he kept his eye on the compass card. We were completely closed in in the wheelhouse; Mandrake and a shadowy figure I took to be the skipper were standing at the rail opposite the doors which led to the deck. The only other way out was a companion which led down from the compass bridge inside the ship.

Charley Fong came up at that moment. He put down a cup of coffee on a ledge in front of the seaman. He just grunted and went on steering. Charley grinned at me; he had a piece of sticking plaster about three inches wide right across the top of his head.

" You want more coffee, Mlistah Faraday?" he asked. I shook my head.

" How's the cranium?" I asked.

" Just fine," he beamed. " Thlanks again."

" Any time," I said. He gave his teeth an airing for the second time and went on down below. Diane Morris leaned across to me. I kept an eye on the helmsman.

" Save the gab for later," I whispered. " This isn't very private."

She nodded and stood up. The helmsman had to get the other side of the wheel to let her get by. She stooped towards me as she slid off the seat.

" I'll try and find out what Mandrake's up to. Charley's on our side. I'll work something out."

" Take it easy—and watch yourself," I told her. She squeezed my hand and went on out through the sliding doors. I sat and smoked and looked at the large expanse of nothing sliding past the cabin windows. From now on in it had to be played by ear; I hoped Clay was going to deal his hand clever. I still had the real bearings if things got really rough. I repeated them over in my head, just to make sure I'd got it right. It would be damned awkward if I forgot them. They were our only tangible form of insurance out here.

The yacht wasn't making much way. The minutes lengthened and still she drove slowly on. We had been under way for more than an hour now. We should have reached the spot, even allowing for the slow speed, but Mandrake might be circling; gaining time or waiting to see if a police boat showed up. I lit another cigarette and stood up, trying to get a look at the compass card but the light was too dim. Besides, it only made the helmsman nervous so I sat down again.

I had been sitting for perhaps ten minutes when footsteps sounded on the lower companion-way and a big form made a rabbit hutch out of the wheelhouse. It was Otto. He hadn't got the gun but he didn't look any less formidable. He grinned. He jerked his thumb.

" Mr. Mandrake wants to see you."

I went down through the big hatch in the floor of the wheelhouse and he followed me down. We went along a familiar corridor and through the sliding doors into the saloon. I heard footsteps on the deck overhead and then the telegraph rang several times in the wheelhouse and the engines slowed and stopped. There was a rattle as the anchor chain went out. The ship started to swing in the low swell.

Mandrake was standing by the big table. He looked as pink and bland as ever. Diane Morris stood and picked nervously at the back of a leather chair. Her blonde hair was like a flame under the light of the saloon lamps. Otto stood behind me. He had got the Luger out now. I could see it from the corner of my eye. Mandrake glanced down at the table before him.

He tapped the little blue book with the names and addresses absently.

" You're sure this is the right spot?" he said. " I wouldn't want there to be any further misunderstandings."

" I'll be diving just as soon as you give the word," I said brightly. More brightly than I was feeling, in fact.

He smiled. He tapped the blue book once again and shook his head.

"I've made up my mind, Mr. Faraday and the evidence is stacked conclusively against you. But for the book we might have made a deal of it. As it is, we're in the place we want to be and you're superfluous baggage. I was never a one for taking unnecessary risks. I've decided to do the diving myself. This is where you get off."

He beckoned to Otto and I felt the gun in my ribs.

"I think the port forward gangway would be the best place," Mandrake told Otto smoothly, as though he were choosing a good lie at golf.

He turned to Diane Morris. "Get below and keep your mouth shut," he told her curtly. She paused as she got opposite me and closed one eyelid as though the light in the saloon was tiring her. Otto was looking at me and didn't see it and she had her back to Mandrake. But as plain as though she'd spelt it out the wink said not to worry. She ran to the door and slammed the sliding panels shut after her. I heard the tattoo of her heels down the corridor.

Otto whistled softly out of the side of his mouth. The Luger moved in a small circle, trained steadily on the spot where it would do most damage. I walked across the saloon in front of him. Mr. Mandrake opened another set of sliding doors and we went out on deck. It was a beautiful night or it would have been had I got the time for such things. Mr. Mandrake led the way forward and I walked in the middle with Otto behind.

I heard a click and a floodlight went on, lighting up the forward gangway. It was the same one where I'd had the fight with Scarpini.

"Walking the plank's a bit corny for this day and age, don't you think?" I said mechanically. It wasn't really a very good effort but then this wasn't my best night. Mandrake didn't answer. He had all the cards and I knew he didn't believe in wasting breath. The stars were very bright and I could hear the clink of knives and forks coming up from the crew's quarters. There was no-one about; they all seemed to be having supper.

Mandrake turned and faced the rail. He looked me over for the last time.

"This will do nicely," he said to Otto. The big man moved towards me, keeping the gun steady and low into his side. His eyes didn't leave my face for a moment. He leaned forward and unhooked the retaining chain at the back of the platform. There was nothing between me and the sea down below.

"Get out on the platform, pal," the big bruiser said gently. He looked almost regretful. "We might as well do this right."

I stepped backwards nice and slow and easy. I didn't want to give him the opportunity of slipping me a slug before it was really the end of the line.

"Good-bye, Mr. Faraday," said Mandrake, an indistinct figure at the rail. "It was an amusing encounter but like everything it had to come to an end some time."

"See you in hell," I said without feeling. Just for the record. To get down on to the platform I had to drop about a foot, edging my way with my heels. The floor of the platform was supported on two L-shaped clamps and the actual deck formed a sort of top step. Otto shifted the angle of the gun downwards; he took it smooth and slow and I knew there was no chance of rushing him.

As I paused I glanced automatically down and along the ship's side. There was a big porthole facing me, just on a level with my feet. I had just got down on to the companionway when a long yellow arm came out of the port, seized my ankle with surprising strength and pulled me to one side. I went over backwards without a sound, clutching at the rail. It wasn't there and I missed. Otto's gun boomed twice, there was a white flash, something scorched my neck and shoulder and then I was turning and falling off the rim of the world. I went down into water and darkness and chaos and death.

CHAPTER TEN

The Island

I

I WAS vomiting. I lay and vomited half the Atlantic Ocean. Water ran out of my mouth, there was nothing but darkness and mottled shapes in front of my eyes and the universe twisted and turned. I tasted salt and blood and burning. I wasn't dead but I began to wish I was.

I closed my eyes again in the roaring darkness and when my head cleared and I stopped retching I could hear voices. I was lying on my face. I opened my eyes to a vagueness. Something touched my shoulder and I felt myself lifted.

" He's conscious," a woman's voice said from far away. Then I saw I was lying in the bottom of a boat; the darkness and mottled shapes were the knots and the graininess of the planking in the boat bottom. That accounted for the rocking too. I still couldn't account for the roaring. Later it translated itself into the sound of a winch.

I sat up. Charley Fong blinked at me in the half-light and grinned encouragingly. He was soaking wet too. The voice belonged to Diane Morris. She sat in the stern of the small row-boat and looked small and scared. Come to think of it she had looked pretty frightened most of the time since this whole thing began, except for our early encounters at the Catamaran.

" What happened?" I said weakly and started coughing again. I struggled up on to one of the wooden bench seats of the boat. It rocked alarmingly and Charley Fong put a steadying hand on my arm.

" Charley fished you out—after tipping you in," Diane said. " We had only a short while and it was all we could think of. I heard Mandrake mention which gangway and then I remembered the big port. It stuck in my mind because it's the place the crew stand to look when women come aboard that way."

I grinned and held out a feeble hand to Charley Fong. " Now it's my turn to say thanks," I said.

" Pleasure," said Charley.

I made my way with difficulty to where Diane sat in the stern.

" Careful," she warned, " you just swallowed half the Atlantic. And keep your voice down."

I started to cough again and she clamped her hand over my mouth. She needn't have worried though. There was the clank and rumble of a winch from overhead and the whine of turbines. I saw we were neatly under the stern of the yacht, right under the overhang, where we couldn't be seen from the deck. Not that anyone was interested; it was pretty dark and all the crew seemed to be where the lights were, up forward. Mandrake was diving for his non-existent treasure.

I began to laugh quietly to myself until my shoulder hurt again. That sobered me up.

I started to take stock. Apart from my feeling weak, the nausea had passed. I felt my shoulder and neck; the flesh stung and I could feel dried blood.

" It's all right," Diane whispered. " Otto missed you, but it was a close thing. As soon as you hit water Charley went in round the stern. I got the dinghy and he fished you out. Everyone was too busy up in the bows."

" They think they finished me?" I asked. She nodded, an indistinct figure, her face a blur of white under even paler-looking hair.

" They checked for half an hour. And they kept flashing the searchlight on every side of the yacht in case the tide had carried you away. But we were already under the stern by then."

I brushed her cheek with my face, felt her lips and kissed her gently.

" Thanks, chum," I said and meant it. She disengaged herself with warm fingers.

" What next?" I asked.

" There's land over there, about half a mile off," she said. " I suggest we row for cover while there's still time. We shan't get two chances. They're so excited over this diving they won't miss me for hours."

" A good idea," I said. " A police cutter will be along before morning, I guess. Incidentally, Mandrake will draw a blank here too."

She laughed. I sat and drank in the night air and the sensation of being alive and felt her shoulders shake under my hands.

" Charley had better get back aboard," I said. " I'll see him right with the police when the time comes. So far as Mandrake knows he's not involved in this; no sense in him sticking his neck out any further. I already owe him a bucketful."

Diane scrambled away from me and went into a whispered conversation with Charley; I could hear some argument going on. Evidently the little man didn't feel like deserting us; common sense prevailed in the end. He slid the boat along by the painter and got his hand over the lower rail. It was dark down here and there was no one about on the deck. I got my cupped hands under the sole of his shoe and heaved him up; the strength was already coming back into my body.

" Thanks again," I said. " We'll pick you up later." I didn't tell him about the police launch. The less he knew about the set-up the better for his safety.

" Slure," he said. He waved down to us and then padded away behind the yacht superstructure. We felt pretty lonely when he'd gone. Diane Morris handed me an oar. I untied the painter and we shoved off. There was a bright moon unfortunately, but if we could get a few hundred yards away unnoticed we'd blend with the shoreline, and there were so many shadows in the tumbled wavelets I hoped we'd pass without comment. I didn't think we'd have to worry as there was so much activity going on up in *The Gay Lady*'s bows, but there was always the odd chance that a seaman might be looking in our direction at the wrong moment.

The current was in our favour and at first we lay on the floorboards to make the boat harder to spot, and let it take us in. I risked a look up over the gunwale after about three minutes to see that we had drifted quite a long way from the yacht; the spotlights on the foredeck burned a vivid yellow hole in the darkness of the night, making a second moon low down on the horizon.

There was a jib hoisted out on the side opposite to us for the diving operations. In front and to one side was the long shape of the land, dark and indistinct, rising from the sea. It was too far off to make out clearly but I could see the faint shimmer where the waves came in on the shore. Diane Morris picked up her oar, I dipped mine in the water and we started to row.

2

A fringe of palms came up the faint sky. The wavelets

tossed us into the shore and the scent of vegetation came out to meet us in the tropic night. It only wanted the Pagan Love Song on the soundtrack and I should have had it made. We rested at the oars and let the tide take us in on to a beach washed pale by the sea and the moon.

I jumped off when we hit the surf and stood in warm water up to my knees; I hauled on the painter and dragged her well up the sand. When she was properly beached Diane Morris came over the gunwale; I scooped her up and carried her up the beach. I felt like Sir Walter Raleigh. Except that when I got close inshore I stubbed my toe on a small outcrop just under the water and we nearly went down on our faces. Sir Walter Raleigh my foot.

I got to the beach in the end and put her down far from gently.

" I didn't think you'd make it, Atlas," she said drily.

" Like I told you I got my muscles coming by post," I said. I was looking around the while; something was wrong but I couldn't spot it for a bit. We went up the beach; it was a lonely place, but the vegetation was thick about a hundred yards in. There were palms, ferns, flowering creepers; we went in under the shadow of the trees.

Any other time this would have been great. We pushed on through the fringe of palms, came out on to more sand; something was still wrong but the nickel didn't drop for another full five minutes. Then I got it. We seemed to have been walking for quite a while but we still couldn't lose the sound of the sea. A few moments more and we came out on to an identical beach. We had arrived at the other side of the island; it was all of a quarter of a mile wide. Five minutes and we were within sight of the boat again. We exchanged long glances. We went back to the dinghy.

" What do you think?" said Diane.

" Seems hardly worth setting off again," I said. " We don't know where the hell we are. Unless you know these waters?"

She shook her head. I took her arm and we walked back along the beach. We went all the way around on the seaward side this time. It took a bit longer but the end result was the same. When we got to the other side there was no land in sight here, no other island. I decided it wasn't worth the risk. We might drift anywhere and Clay would pick us up at the rendezvous in due course; he only had two known bearings and we had to be at one of these.

The thing which worried me most was that Mandrake might find Diane had disappeared too soon; he would be pretty mad when he found only sand on the bottom and I didn't want her to be around when that happened. In that case he could hardly fail to spot the boat and then he would know I wasn't making fish-bait. But it wasn't worth busting a gut for. It was a great night and a blonde and a desert island wouldn't make it too hard to bear.

I went and felt the gunwhale of the dinghy. It was much bigger out of the water and heftily built; solid teak for the most part, I guessed. There didn't seem much chance of the two of us dragging it up the beach and behind the trees. And even then there would be the marks in the sand to erase. I thought about it for a bit longer and then decided to let it go. It wasn't worth it, especially as Mandrake would know the boat was missing and the island was the only place the girl could be. No-one but a nut case would row off into nowhere in these waters. And she was no nut case.

The problem became academic a few moments after. A beam of light shot across the water and there was the deep throb of a marine engine as a small cutter came across the bay. I glanced up beyond the dinghy and saw that the boat was well away from the yacht, the small searchlight in the bow cutting the dusk into segments as it moved in a complete circle.

The light moved on over us, steadied, came back and then remained stationary on the dinghy. I could almost feel night glasses being focussed in our direction. As the beam pencilled on down the beach I grabbed Diane and we made a run for the trees. Against the white sand of the beach we didn't stand a chance of going without being observed. The light came back again and held us pinned as we ran in an almost straight line through the fine, powdery sand.

I heard a shout, " There's two of them," and the sound of a shot; there was a vicious whang and sand scattered in puffs at the edge of the beach, down near the dinghy. Then we were in among the trees. The firing stopped and there was a moment's silence. This was followed by the metallic whine of a loud-hailer. After the preliminary crackle there was Otto's voice.

" Well, well, pal. You're kinda durable at that. Better come on out while there's a chance."

I risked a glance through the fringe of undergrowth; Diane's frightened breathing sounded close to me. I could feel her trembling through the contact of her hand on my arm. The boat creamed in to the shallows and dark figures got down on to the beach. They fussed around the dinghy. If they came up to us we were finished; we could play hide and seek among the trees for half an hour, but there didn't seem much percentage in it.

There was a delay of about ten minutes and then I saw lights flashing from the yacht; I never learned to read Morse so I missed an interesting conversation. The cutter used the searchlight to reply. There was another pause and then a final short message from *The Gay Lady*. Darkness closed in again.

The engine of the cutter started up and she put out to sea towing the dinghy. It bobbed in her wake and I saw one of the seamen get down in the stern to let out the painter. The loudhailer crackled again. Otto sounded amused.

" We'll pick you up in the morning, pal. You ain't goin' any place. Make the most of it."

The engine of the cutter died in the distance and then there was nothing but the sound of the surf. Diane Morris turned towards me and quietly came into my arms. I held her close.

3

The moon looked like a silver nickel cut out of the darkness of the sky. It was warm enough to be comfortable. I lay back on the soft sand, stretched out my clasped hands behind my head and looked up at the stars. I would have given a lot for a cigarette just then. The fellows on the TV programmes always leave out bits like that when they talk about life on desert islands. Who the hell wants phonograph records when there's women around? I'll settle for a blonde any time.

Diane moved at my side. I waited until she'd settled herself more comfortably again and then looked back up at the sky. Its remoteness made Mandrake and the whole mess seem unimportant. It would be the thing to get out for Diane Morris. She had done quite a deal for me in the last twenty-four hours. At least I owed her that. And anyways I was hoping the police cutter would turn up soon. It seemed a long while since I had seen Stella. I stopped thinking then. The recollection of her face took the edge off my plans for tonight.

I sat and stretched myself. A soft wind was stirring the tops of the palms. I stood, shook the sand out of my trousers and stared out to sea. I couldn't see the yacht any more but I knew it was still there. Suddenly I felt tired of this side of the island. Diane Morris had woken. She lay staring at me. I could see the moonlight glinting on her half-opened eyes. I guessed the time was only around eleven o'clock and I didn't feel like sleeping. I'd never felt less like sleeping in my life.

" Nickel for them," she said. I grinned. I grabbed her by the hand and hauled her to her feet.

" Come on," I said. " It's a lovely night for a walk."

She leaned against me and looked up into my face. Her eyes were smiling.

" You sure that's all you had in mind?" she said.

" It's too public this side," I said.

" Let's go, then," she replied.

We walked back up through the glades, silver bright in the moon; each leaf and frond and branch looked like an old steel engraving in that light. She walked close to me and I put one hand on her shoulder. We didn't talk. She was so close I could get the perfume of her hair. It smelt better than the trees and flowers around us. At last we came out of the last clump of trees and the sea lay blank before us, pricked with tiny points of light where the moonlight brushed the surface.

" I know where the money is," I told Diane as we sat down where a shelf of rock ran out before dying as a spit in the sand. It made a sort of hollow cup in the shore and it still held all the heat of the day. The sand was fine and silver-pink with the conch shells and the warmth came up off the sand like the gentle heat of a baker's oven when the fire has died. She folded her hands across her body and lay on the sand.

" I guessed you did," she said gravely. " So?"

" So this," I said. " Mandrake's going to be pretty sore in the morning. Both at you and me. Me mostly but you also, especially for tonight's caper."

She turned her face away from me and looked out across the water. I couldn't see the expression of her eyes. She ran one hand aimlessly through the fine sand, letting it sift through her slender fingers.

" I've got the real position where the money's stashed," I said. " So have the police so it doesn't make any odds now whether Mandrake knows or not. They'll be waiting for him in any case—they may even be here by morning. This was the alternative rendezvous."

" You never intended to play ball at any time, did you?" she said.

" What do you think?" I asked. She laughed.

" That I'm a pretty good judge of character. Once a cop and all that. Not that I blame you. Mandrake's not a very attractive person. But I thought the five thousand might tempt you."

" Disappointed?" I said.

She shook her head. " No," she said. I leaned over and kissed her. She lay quietly and rode with it. The sand seemed to be swaying to the motion of the sea. I put my hand out and grabbed the rock in the end, just to stop us from floating out with the tide. She broke for air then and passed her hand over her face in a lazy movement. We lay for a moment drinking in the night. She seemed to be thinking over what I had just said.

But in the end all she said was, " You kiss pretty good for a cop."

" It's one of the tests we have to pass before we get our badge," I said. She chuckled again.

" Look, Diane," I said. " I'll give you the map reference if you think you can memorise it. It's my ace in the pack for the morning. But just in case Mandrake doesn't believe me—and I can't see that happening after today—it will make all the difference if things get rough. Besides, Otto may shoot first and interrogate me afterwards."

She trembled in my arms. She didn't reply.

" You listening?" I said. She started.

" Sorry."

" Now get this," I said. I gave her the bearings, repeated them twice more. I needn't have worried though. She got them first time off.

" Thanks, Mike," she said. " I'll see Mandrake first thing. He wants me to marry him. I'll do what I can."

" Stow that," I said putting my hand over her mouth.
" The cost of some things comes too high."

She smiled. " And I thought you were cynical," she
said. " Don't tell me you're jealous?"

" Not tonight," I said. " Tonight I got all the aces."

We kissed again. She leaned towards me on the warm
sand and all the front of her body came along mine; we
lay toe to toe. It felt pretty good.

" Let's make a night of it," she breathed.

" It's a pity I didn't bring my pocket chess set," I said.

" Quit the kidding," she said almost savagely. White
teeth nipped at my ear. I started to get serious then. It
wasn't very hard. She had on some sort of open-necked
shirt which exposed the muscles of her neck. I had trouble
with the buttons of the shirt. In the end she gently moved
my hands and unbuttoned it herself; she was kind of impatient at that. I thought she was pretty striking when I
saw her in my hotel room but that was a dry run compared
to this.

She had a pair of breasts that weren't exactly hard to
look at. They were the best kind; they don't make them
like that any more. They never did. I'm not very good at
sizes but they just fitted my hands. Diane moaned then.
By this time I was getting reckless with the tropical night
and all; I just pulled all her clothes off and we got down
to business.

She squealed as we rolled over the warm sand but she
wasn't frightened; I'll say she wasn't. I found her mouth
and then we were locked together; the warmth of her body
all along mine would have set fire to the sand if it had been
inflammable. And I was already ablaze by that time; an
asbestos saint would have been hard put to it and I wasn't
even a plaster one. Smothered with sand and passion we
rolled down into a hollow. She bit my ear again.

" You can do anything you like," she said.

" I'm always ready to oblige a lady," I said. I obliged.

4

When we woke the moon was high, riding way up the sky and silvering the wave-tips. Diane stood up and undulated her fingertips across my face. Stark naked, she was a fine sight in the light of the moon; her white skin made pale strips which her bikini usually covered. For the rest she looked like a bronze goddess as she laughed down at me.

She ran down the beach and I pounded after her. The way we dashed into the spray made Dante and Beatrice look like a couple of old-age pensioners. I figured Clay would have had apoplexy if he could have seen us. Or perhaps he wouldn't.

I didn't get time to examine the subject for Diane caught me behind the calf with her foot and I went down with a splutter into the water. It was as soft and smooth as warm milk. We horsed around in the shallows for a bit. She swam beautifully, like an athlete; she had me outclassed easily, but tonight she wasn't trying to get away. I had no difficulty in catching her.

Her body was as smooth as marble under the water but wonderfully alive. We rolled up the foamy shallows into the wet sand laughing and pinching like a couple of twelve-year olds. Her wet hair fell across my eyes as we kissed. I held her warm flanks in my two hands and held her tight against me. We kissed as the tide drove us roughly in over the sand. I cupped her buttocks and held her close. We were kissing deeply and it felt like we were dropping through the water into oblivion. What a way to drown I thought.

She whispered in my ear. Her voice was full of wonder.

" I've never done it under water, Mike," she said.

" There's a first time for everything," I said, like I did it every day before breakfast. It looked like being a long night before the dawn came up.

CHAPTER ELEVEN

Piranha

I

A PALE shaft of light fell across my closed eyelids. A red glow was suffusing the shadowy surface of the sea when I opened them. Diane stirred at my side.

"Dawn," I said. She nodded. A light wind came from off the water and rustled the palms. Down on the sand here it was still warm and the rocks protected us from the breeze. I sat up and stretched.

"Time to go," I said. She got up then and held out her arms. I held her against me.

"Thanks for everything," I said. "Not to worry."

She put her face against mine. "I'll do what I can," she whispered. "I'll do what I can."

I pushed her gently away and she gave me a faint smile. Then we set out to walking round the island. The light was growing stronger and the water looked phosphorescent as the slight swell came in from the ocean. The dawn tints on the reddish colour of the sand made the light look very beautiful. White clouds painted orange by the rising sun hung on the horizon.

We soon came in sight of the yacht. It rode on the surface

F

of the water looking like a painted ship on a painted back-cloth; I swung my eyes the whole hundred and seventy-five degrees of the horizon but there wasn't a sign of Clay's police cutter. Nothing but the white triangle of a fishing boat, almost hull down, far out to sea. Diane sighed. It wasn't worth a comment.

We went up from the water aways and sat down on some rocks. Presently I heard the sound of an outboard and a dinghy put out from *The Gay Lady*. The sun was pretty well up now and I could recognise the big form of Otto in the stern. Diane gave me a long, last look and then went down the beach to meet the boat. I followed on behind.

The dinghy grounded in the shallows and one of the seamen jumped ashore and hauled her in. Otto got out and came through the surf to meet us. In the stern the steersman had dropped the tiller and sat with a shotgun across his knees.

"You're a lousy shot," I told Otto. He creased up his face but whether with humour or disgust I couldn't make out. He spat on to the sand.

"You were lucky, pal," he said. "It won't happen again."

He didn't have the Luger out but it wasn't worth trying anything with the three of them there. We wouldn't have stood a chance.

Otto jerked his head at Diane Morris. "Mr. Mandrake wants to see you aboard—right now."

She looked round the island in one brief glance, flashed me a quick smile and went down to the boat. I went to follow but Otto put a big hand against my chest.

"You stay here, pal," he said. "Mr. Mandrake's got something special laid on for you."

"How'd he make out with the treasure?" I said.

Otto shook his head. "Bad, pal, bad," he said softly. "He's pretty mad at you."

"I never was much good at remembering things," I said.

Otto chuckled way down in his throat. He motioned me up the beach. I went back and sat on a rock. He sat about two yards away from me. I looked down to the shore. The boat was half-way across now. Diane Morris looked very small in the stern. She stared in front of her without looking back.

Otto got out a pack of cigarettes. He took the Luger out of his pocket, took off the safety catch and laid it down near his hand. The scrape of the match made a thin, irritating sound in the dawn quiet. He feathered out the smoke with satisfaction.

" Do you mind?" I said. He looked across at me.

" Why not?"

He threw the cigarettes and the box of matches across to me. They fell in the sand by my feet. I picked them up very slowly and lit a cigarette. I threw back the box and the package. Otto let them lie where they fell. I drew in a lungful of smoke and looked up to the tops of the palms. The smoke tasted good.

We sat there for perhaps thirty minutes; Otto didn't say anything but his eyes never left my face. Myself, I didn't feel like talking. Then I heard the sound of the motor again. The dinghy was coming back. I could see Diane Morris in the stern and a bigger-built bulk which could only be Mandrake. Midships the boat was taken up by a large, square shape which glinted in the sun.

Mandrake got out of the boat and came up the beach towards us. Diane Morris followed, carrying a large metal case. The two seamen started unloading the dinghy; they had some trouble with their burden. It was a large, plate glass fish tank like the ones I had seen in *The Gay Lady* saloon, only bigger. Otto picked up his Luger and motioned to me to stand.

Mandrake eyed me coldly. He was wearing a white drill suit which made his pink hands look even more incongruous than usual. Only his eyes looked alive in his pink-scrubbed features; they were burning with hatred just now but his face remained coldly immobile.

" Looks like you got your bearings mixed up," I said mildly.

Mandrake hit me across the face three times rapidly; I rocked with the blows and instinctively bunched my fists but Otto had the Luger swiftly at my navel. I tasted blood inside my mouth.

" I have finished with talking, Mr. Faraday," said Mandrake savagely. " Already too much time, energy and money has been wasted over your stupid interference. You have been extraordinarily lucky but luck runs out even for the boldest. Last night you could have died with the minimum of pain and inconvenience. This morning I regret to say that I shall demand a large dividend for the trouble you have put me. Now your death will be slow and extremely painful."

Diane Morris put down the metal case. She didn't look at me.

" Sounds like some fun," I said. " You know the real location of the money now, so why all the fireworks?"

He pointed one of his pink starfish at my face.

" We have only your word for that, Mr. Faraday and so far I have found you extremely unreliable."

" My word against the girl's safety," I said.

" The time is past for bargains," he said. " The girl will take her chances. You will die in any case."

I shrugged. " There's no need to involve her in this," I said.

He turned and gazed out thoughtfully towards the pale-blue of the horizon.

" She is already involved," he said absently. " But in any case we shall be far away when the time comes. Your solicitude is really touching."

He stared towards the rim of the sea where the faintest white triangle of the fishing boat slowly faded from sight.

When it had disappeared he turned back to me.

" You may remember a conversation we had some while ago concerning Chinese river pirates and their unpleasant habits. Unfortunately I have no facilities for that sort of elaborate set-up here. But we will make shift with the next best thing."

He motioned to Otto. The big man gestured with the Luger.

" Take off that sweater, pal," he said. " And your shoes. You won't be needing them any more."

I obeyed. When I had stripped to the waist the two seamen came up with the big plate glass tank. It had a metal frame and must have been heavy judging by the sweat which was running down their faces.

" Put it down here behind these rocks," said Mandrake. " Now, Mr. Faraday, I must ask you to put your hands behind your back."

When I had done this one of the seamen came up behind me and roped my hands together. He made a pretty good job of it. Then he soaked the rope with sea water. When he had checked it again Mandrake came up behind me and tested it for himself.

" Now the feet," he said softly. When the two seamen had finished with me I looked like a trussed chicken. Otto sat on the rock with the Luger and gave me a satisfied glance. Then they brought up several big rocks and tied these to the ropes round my feet. I couldn't move. In fact I had difficulty in standing.

" You'll have to do better than this," I told Mandrake. " Houdini was my uncle."

He gave me a dry look. " You have an admirable spirit, Mr. Faraday, which has been grossly misapplied until now. However, this experiment will give your stoicism an opportunity to manifest itself."

As he spoke the two seamen came up behind and started to lift me; they couldn't do it. Otto got up. He took my

feet and the weight of the rocks. They were big ones and
they made him grunt. The three men lifted me into the fish
tank. I cut my injured shoulder on the top as I went over
and blood ran down the glass.

"Careful, you fools," said Mandrake sharply. "If you
drop him the rocks will break the glass and we shall have
to start all over."

The seamen and Otto lowered me inch by inch. When
they stood away I was securely anchored to the floor of the
tank by the weights round my feet. With my hands behind
my back I was wedged up in the angle of one of the corners;
I might as well have been in solid concrete for all the free-
dom of movement it left me. The ugly seaman got a bucket
out of the dinghy. He came back and slopped the water
into the bottom of the tank. It felt warm on my feet.

Mandrake sighed heavily. "You get more stupid all the
time," he told the seaman. "The four of you make a chain
and pass the bucket up the beach. It will take all day the
way you are doing it."

Otto got up grumbling from his seat on the rock but
changed his expression when Mandrake looked over at him.
He went down the beach with surprising speed. As the
buckets of water slopped into the tank and the water began
to rise up to my ankles Mandrake stood looking reflectively
down at me.

"We will stop when the water gets up to your navel,"
he said. "By avoiding any vital parts you will last a lot
longer. It will give you plenty of time to reflect on the
mistakes you have made over the last two days. You may
perhaps have wondered at the metal can the girl was
carrying. It contains the fish that interested you so much on
the yacht. The Serrasalmus—or to the layman, the piranha.
As you saw I have only half a dozen so it should take
quite a while for them to work through you. They are
gorged with food at the moment, but when they get
hungry . . ."

He waved a pink starfish in the air and stared at me again. " You look a husky specimen, Mr. Faraday," he said. " A tempting morsel to such game little fellows. They should be able to live off you for weeks. But you'll be all right for a bit—until they get hungry, that is. As I said before, my only regret is that I shan't be here to see it. I'm told that a man can snap inch manila rope when they get stuck into him but the rocks will hold you safely. My only fear is that you will drown before the process is complete."

No-one spoke for a moment. Diane Morris walked a few yards off and even Otto had lost his smile. For once I couldn't think of a crack. I thought of the cat back in *The Gay Lady*'s saloon and I began to sweat. The water was up over my thighs now but still the last few buckets kept coming. The two seamen and Otto spread out farther Diane Morris came and stood near the edge of the tank. She still didn't look at me.

At last Mandrake raised his hand and the ugly seaman who had the shotgun thankfully put the last pail of water into the tank. He walked off with the empty bucket back to the boat. I looked at Mr. Mandrake for a long, silent moment. Mr. Mandrake from Chicago.

" Hog Butcher to the World," I said softly.

" What was that?" he barked.

" Nothing," I said. " Leastways, nothing you'd understand."

Otto went off then. He spat on the sand as he went by. He strode off down the beach taking the other seaman with him. The dinghy stood by.

Mandrake jerked his head at Diane Morris. " Now," he said.

She picked up the metal canister. I saw that the top had holes pierced in it. Keeping her head averted she poured the contents into the tank. The water was full of sand which clouded the tank immediately but through the misty water

I could see and feel the darting shapes of the small red fish.

Mandrake tapped the glass with a sensuous expression on his face.

" Lay off the girl," I said. " I was going to kill you anyway but if you fool with her you'll prefer the fish-tank to what I'll dream up for you."

He laughed. " I think not, Mr. Faraday."

" See you around," I said.

" Good-bye," said Mr. Mandrake.

Diane Morris went off at a half-run down the beach. Mandrake picked up the metal can and followed her. I saw them get in the dinghy. A moment or two later the motor crackled and then they took off. I was alone.

2

When I felt the body of the first fish dart against me in the sandy water I drew in my belly muscles so far back I felt they must meet my spine. But when the initial fear had left me I was curiously calm; I remembered what Mandrake had said about their feeding habits but the image of that damn cat kept coming back into my mind.

I focussed my eyes up into the tree tops and concentrated on other things; principally where the hell Clay had got to and what the Stanley Bay Police Force were doing. Sweat ran into my eyes despite the general coolness of the water in the tank. By twisting my head I could just see the yacht; the muted note of engines came across the water. She was putting out to sea. It looked like Mandrake was going for the money and I could only hope Clay would be waiting for him. At least that would be some satisfaction, even if I wouldn't be there to see it.

I tested the ropes behind me, but they were too well tied; my legs were numb and though my body weighed little in the water the roping had been done by experts and the rocks were far too big and heavy. After all I had seen they took three men to lift when they put me in here. I flexed up my muscles but the only immediate reaction was another trickle of blood running down the rough bandage Diane had put across my injured shoulder.

I looked up into the trees again and forced myself to think of other matters. I didn't blame Diane Morris; she had her own life to think of and she couldn't have done anything against the four men. I wondered how she would play her cards if Clay caught up with them; I hoped he would give her a decent break.

I felt something flicker against my inner thigh and the vibration of tiny fins set the nerves creeping up my body; I tightened my jaw and my flesh instinctively shrank away from fibrillating shapes that surrounded me, invisible in the tank. I had to give Mandrake full marks for a good idea—right out of the comic strips. It was just about his mark; corny and fiendish at the same time.

But he had got me going; I'm fairly steady in most situations but this was something new for me. A fly buzzed in the silence; it settled on the edge of the tank. A big, bloated blowfly with a metallic blue body; the sweat ran down my face again and I licked my cracked lips. I hoped to Christ it wouldn't settle on my head. The place would be full of blowflies if these fish got hungry.

Thinking about comic strips set my mind in parallel curves; if this was a Popeye film he would get the blasted fish to eat through the ropes instead of the victim. For some reason this seemed like a hell of a joke to me; there was a strange sound and the blowfly flew away. Then I heard myself laughing and shut up with a start; I must have been a little delirious or maybe it was the heat.

The outlines of the tank and the sand beyond kept getting blurry and I sagged against the side; the tightness of the ropes was beginning to tell and they were stopping the circulation. This was more serious than the long-term hazards; if I got dizzy and fell forward I shouldn't be able to get up again. I should drown before the piranha got their dinner. There was a thought. Anyway, it would be better than what Mandrake had planned. I could try that if it came to the pinch, though I had heard that it was the most difficult thing in the world to drown yourself deliberately.

I opened my eyes and when I turned my head I saw that the yacht had gone; the sun was well up. I couldn't tell whether an hour had passed or two. All time seemed the same in this situation. If I had passed out for a bit it may well have been more than an hour. If Mandrake had gone full speed he could be diving by now. Or would he play it clever for another day and cruise about a bit and pick up the money after nightfall? I estimated if he had believed our story he would contain his impatience and have a go after dark; a big yacht mounting full-scale diving operations in daylight was asking for trouble with the stakes he was playing for.

I bit my tongue as something slipped and slithered along my groin. I had a job to keep from calling out. I could feel my nerve going. Every minute or so these things bumped me in their aimless to and fro; it was a joke to think that a thing smaller than a self-respecting herring could be so lethal. If I hadn't been in Mandrake's saloon that afternoon I might not have been so worried; but not after that.

It was when the violins began to play that I knew I was losing my mind; it was a symphony or something and the tune kept getting louder in my head. The sweat was in my eyes now and the blaze of the sun and the scarlet spreading on my shoulder made a vivid pattern whenever I opened them; I moved my head and the violins stopped. But when I settled back again the music began once more. I opened my eyes and saw who was playing the violins. The blow-fly had collected some of his friends and they were having a concert. They probed delicately at the blood on my bandaged shoulder and waited for me to die. I laughed again then but I guess I was too crazy to care.

The heat of the sun was splitting my head open and I'd even stopped moving my stomach whenever a piranha nudged against it. I knew I couldn't last much longer and for the first time I didn't really care. The piranha had the heads of blowfies now and they were all playing as they sat down to table. I couldn't recognise the tune but is sounded like something grand and funereal. Tough luck Faraday I told myself. Too bad to get it on holiday. That was a joke. Stella would be pleased.

When I thought about Stella that sobered me up. Irritation became uppermost in my mind and then anger; at Mandrake, the fish, the tank, the ropes that were slicing into me and most of all at the moment, the blowflies. I shook my head savagely and slopped the water with my body. My head cleared and I could see the stretch of beach. There was something white blocking my view; something white and billowing which moved across the field of vision.

The death-horn blew and then the universe split and flew into fragments. Water, glass and consciousness dissolved and I was one with the whirling sky. I went down into warm sand and salt water washed over me. I lay dazed, surprised to find myself still alive.

A shadow blocked out the sun. Something pink blinked into existence over my shoulder.

" Sorry about this, old man," said Ian Phillips throwing down his rifle and kneeling by my side. " We've had one hell of a night !"

CHAPTER TWELVE

Exit a Blonde

I

I SWIGGED my third cup of coffee and listened to Colonel
Clay apologise again.

" I can't tell you how sorry I am, my dear chap," he
said. He sat across from me in the cabin of the police patrol
boat and looked at me with concern. Stella sat next to me
with a curiously flushed face and held my hand. Phillips
dabbed at my shoulder with an iodine pad.

" We've had the most frightful night," said Clay. " We
made the mistake of going to the real rendezvous first in
order to intercept. Then the engine broke down and that
took until dawn to fix. We got here on half-revs. If Ian
hadn't commandeered this fishing boat I don't know what
would have happened."

" Not to worry," I said. " I'd only been in the tank for
two or three hours."

Stella shuddered.

" Until then," Clay went on, " things had been fine.
We had the yacht pin-pointed by two radar stations and we
had reports of her position every half hour. We were able
to keep a check on your movements at all times. Though
that didn't help much when the engine went out."

He rubbed his chin ruefully and stared out over the sparkling water. We were anchored just off shore and the fishing boat he had been talking about lay in the surf two hundred yards from us while its two-man Bahamian crew sat in the sun and mended nets. It was their white sail I had seen when I was half out of my head and Ian Phillips had risked a shot with his rifle, shattering the tank at the end farthest from me and tipping the whole thing over when the water ran out. That reminded me I hadn't congratulated him on his shooting. I owed him a lot.

"Thanks for the William Tell stuff," I said. "I guess it wasn't my day to make piranha bait."

Phillips put a new bandage on my shoulder, tightened the last knot and turned to me with a puzzled look.

"I don't get it," he said. My turn to be confused.

"It was Mandrake's idea to feed me to the fishes," I said.

He grinned. "I wondered what the gimmick was. You were in no danger of anything except drowning."

He picked up a tin out of the stern of the boat. "It seemed a shame to waste these little fellows. They're worth about a pound apiece in the open market."

He put his hand into the tin and stroked the small pink forms which milled about inside. "Ordinary tropical fish," he said. "Someone's been having you on. Only thing these would frighten is a mealworm."

Clay's face was a picture and mine must have mirrored his for Stella suddenly burst out laughing. I put on the shirt Clay handed me as I puzzled at it. Then I understood why Diane Morris had put so much sand in the water; she wanted it cloudy so Mandrake wouldn't tumble to the switch.

"The girl changed the fish over," I told Clay. "She told me last night she'd do the best she could for me."

I looked at him quietly. "I think she's earned an amnesty," I told him.

He nodded slowly. " I'll go along with that, Michael," he said. " Mandrake and his friends are the ones we're after."

I pointed over to the fishing boat. " Have we still got the use of this?" I asked.

Clay looked at Phillips and then back at me.

" She's commandeered until further orders for police duties," he said. " What have you got on your mind?"

" An idea," I said. " We shall need the fishing boat to carry it out tonight."

Clay looked hesitant but it was Stella who put it into the open.

" Don't you think you've done enough, Mike?" she said. " Why not leave it to Colonel Clay and the regular police?"

" Sensible words," I said. " It's not that I'm being heroic but this has become a personal thing between Mandrake and me. If we go barging in there with police launches and rifles things will start popping and someone's bound to get hurt apart from the girl. And I've a debt to her which I'd like to repay myself."

Clay eyed me dubiously. " The young lady's right, you know, Michael. It's all right with me if you want to play it like that. I think you've earned it with the way you've handled things so far. But I insist that Phillips shall be with you at all times. I almost wish we'd come in last night when we saw you go overboard. It was touch and go."

" I'm glad you didn't," I said. " It would have spoiled everything and Mandrake may well have gotten away with it. Any premature move by the police would have defeated the exercise."

Clay frowned and picked up his half-empty coffee-cup. " Anyway, I decided to let things take their course when we saw you come back aboard. If we hadn't had all this engine trouble the case would have been closed by now. Are you sure you feel up to tackling things?"

" I'll be all right by tonight," I said. " I don't think
Mandrake will make any direct move to lift the money
until after dark. You got any reports on their position?"

He took out a sheet of paper from his inside jacket
pocket. " They've been zig-zagging in a wide circle about
twenty miles from here for the last hour," he said. " I'm
inclined to agree, Michael. If what you surmise is correct,
after nightfall would be the best course. We'll work that
out after we've eaten."

" Was that you I saw just after dawn?" I asked Phillips.

He smiled again. " That was Stella's idea," he said.
" She insisted on coming with me when we hailed the fishing
boat at two this morning. We installed the spare radio and
transmitter to keep in touch with Colonel Clay and cruised
around this position. I edged in as close as we could at
dawn but kept away when I saw Mandrake and all that
crowd on the beach. I stooged along to the other side of
the island and when we saw the yacht go away we came
back. I must say it made a rather fine finish to a pretty
rough night."

" You can say that again," I said.

A native constable poked his head in at the hatch.
" Another message just in, sir," he said to Clay. " Yacht
continues to zig-zag. Same circular course as before."

" Thank you," said Clay perfunctorily. " Acknowledge."
The constable saluted and withdrew his head.

" So far so good," said Clay. " I'll have another patrol
boat standing by at Stanley Bay tonight and we'll rendezvous on my signal. We'll discuss this fishing boat scheme
of yours over a meal, Michael."

We sat thankfully down round the small cabin table.

2

It was dusk. Stella and I sat in the stern of the patrol boat and watched the yellows and reds chasing the greens and blues out of the darkening sky. The sea made a dazzle of molten silver in the fading light. She put her head quietly against my face and her arms tightened about me.

"You'll take care, won't you, Mike?" she said gently. "You know, the last week hasn't been much of a holiday for me."

"I know, honey," I said. "After tonight things will be the same as before. You'll see."

"I hope so," she said. She kissed me again and then pulled away.

"Not to worry," I said. A form materialised in the gloom behind us and I heard Clay's apologetic cough.

"Time to go in about half an hour," he said. "Let me know when you want to go aboard the fishing-boat. We'd better check our watches."

As he called out the seconds, we synchronised them against Phillips'. I bet the old boy had been in his element during the last war. Anyway, it pleased him. Phillips was ready to go, so we ran through the arrangements for the last time.

"What about armaments?" I asked.

"Phillips has a revolver," said the Colonel. "I think it's best to leave things at that. After all, you are a civilian. You've come out all right so far in tougher situations. We hold all the cards tonight and I think one revolver is enough."

I didn't argue with that. After all it was his show now and the way I felt tonight I could handle Mandrake with my bare hands. In fact it would give me more pleasure that way.

"You've got the waterproofs?" he asked Phillips.

"Everything here, sir," said the Inspector, tapping a bundle he carried.

"Off you go, then," said Clay gruffly. He waited until Phillips had dropped overside into the dinghy which a con-

stable was manning amidships. He held out his hand
to me in the dusk. " See you later, then, Michael."

" Fine," I said. " Remember, give us half an hour after
we hit *The Gay Lady*. We've got to get into position first
before we know which way to play it. And I want to make
sure the girl gets a square deal. I figure Mandrake won't
start diving until well after dark. That will make it around
ten. With this wind we should get aboard, with a little
luck, around ten-thirty. If you lay a couple of miles off and
then come in soon after eleven you should be about right."

Clay nodded. I went over the side and down into the
dinghy. Stella's face was a pink blur in the light of the
setting sun. She waved as I went down.

" I'll test the radio, sir, as soon as we get aboard," said
Phillips. Then we dropped away from the side of the police
launch in the choppy tide. The constable rowed rapidly
and in a very few moments we jumped out in the surf of
Stocking Island. The constable set back and Phillips and
I splashed through the surf to the fishing boat; two natives
with broad grins above their tattered shirts helped us over
the gunwale.

I stepped down into a dark space in the tween-decks
where the dim light of a lantern glinted on the metal con-
tours of a heavy duty radio transmitter. The boat lurched
and I could hear the soft thud of ropes in blocks as the
two-man crew hoisted sail. I put down my gear in a corner
which smelt of fish and lit a cigarette, while Phillips tested
the radio.

" All well," he grunted after a minute. " The Colonel
says *bon voyage*."

We went out on deck again as the boat surged forward
over the tide, heading towards the horizon where the sunset
burned itself out in the depths of the sea. A light winked
from the police launch and we could see the heads of Clay
and Stella. They waved as we went by. Then we were
clear of the land and the mast creaked and the sail

thrummed as the breeze caught her and drove us on into the west with an exhilaration known only to those who sail small boats.

One of the boatmen was up tightening the foresail, while the other hummed tunelessly at the tiller as he straightened up on course. I stood for a moment smoking and looking at the wild beauty of the night sky and then back at the fading silhouette of the police boat.

" They know exactly where we're going," said Phillips, answering my unspoken query. " They know these waters like I know Stanley Bay parking regulations."

While the boat thrust on through the small chop which was setting out from the islands, Phillips and I got ready for the evening's entertainment. I stripped into a pair of sharkskin swimming trunks but kept my thick shirt on. I wore a belt over the top of the shirt and trunks and there was a useful knife in a rubber sheath attached to the belt. I stowed my watch in a waterproof bag Phillips had fixed to his wrist with a piece of webbing.

He also had his revolver and spare ammunition in there; that was additionally wrapped in oiled silk with another rubberised waterproof bag round that. I guessed he must have been in Combined Operations during the war. Then I did some arithmetic and decided he was too young. He'd been trained well, though, I gave him that.

By this time the boat was making a fair pace and the light had faded almost entirely from the sky. The breeze was fresh out here and the sea had an unearthly beauty as it caught and flung back the last of the brightness from the horizon. We had finished our preparations and we sat in the lee of the mast and smoked. The two owners of the boat sat at the tiller and talked in quiet voices. I dozed off for a while. When I woke it was quite dark and the only light came from the swaying lantern in the cubby-hole up forward. I stumbled back in to find Phillips at the set.

"All well," he said. "Police boat starting off in a few more minutes."

"Let's hope the engine holds out all right this time," I said grimly.

"No worries tonight," he said. "The sergeant fitted the spare pump this afternoon."

I sat down on a low bench inside the cabin and finished my cigarette. Something dark and soft rubbed against my leg. I got hold of the lantern and by its re-directed light I saw red eyes and white teeth. A large black cat sat blinking up at me.

"Good luck," said Phillips facetiously.

It gave me an idea. "We'll take it with us," I said.

Phillips looked at me uncomprehendingly. "What the hell for?" he said.

"It'll shorten the odds," I said. He laughed as I explained. Then he went up forward and rooted around among the assorted junk. One of the boatmen came and joined us. I told him what we wanted and he helped Phillips in the search. By the time we were organised we were almost at the rendezvous. I came on deck again to find a thin cone of light low down the horizon just off the port bow.

"*Gay Lady?*" Phillips breathed at my elbow. I nodded. Phillips went aft to talk to the boatmen and a few minutes later they started to slacken sail and the boat began to lose way. We stubbed out our cigarettes and silently watched as the mushroom of light grew nearer.

The boatmen had been well briefed and they made a good job of our approach. We only wanted to leave a few hundred yards for swimming and we relied on the boat itself to distract the yacht's crew. Once alongside we could rely on luck to get aboard.

When Phillips judged we were in the right position he whispered back to the helmsman. "Now," he said to me. I went over the starboard gunwale, the side farthest from the yacht. The water was surprisingly warm and I felt less exposed down here. Then he passed me down the cat. I felt a bit mean about this but we had assured the owner of its safety.

We had a big canvas lifebelt. Lashed across the bottom of this we had slats of wood for the cat to stand on. The animal itself was secured to the improvised life raft with thin cord round its neck. Cats don't like water anyway, so I knew it wouldn't try to jump over. Just in case it felt like singing I had my hand over its mouth.

It behaved pretty well under the circumstances. As soon as I got clear of the boat I started swimming towards the dim bulk of the yacht. The tide was setting in that direction, which is what we had planned. After a moment the cat lost its uneasiness and stood cautiously in the water swilling about inside the lifebelt. But it didn't make a sound.

I looked back over my shoulder and saw Phillips' head bobbing about behind me. He was a powerful swimmer so I didn't wait for him but pushed ahead with my bundle and the cat and the inspector soon caught up with me.

" No problems," he said as he came alongside. I shook my head and spat out salt water.

" We'll make it all right," I told him. We slacked off momentarily and watched the sail of the fishing boat chopping the night. *The Gay Lady*'s foredeck was brilliantly lit with floodlamps and we could hear pumps going. The boom was out on the port side, the side away from us, which was where I hoped Mandrake would be diving. The sailboat set out to cross several hundred yards ahead of *The Gay Lady*'s bows, as we had arranged. Then a searchlight stabbed the sea, held the big sail in its white light and a loud-hailer crackled, " Fishing boat, ahoy."

A voice weaker and distorted by a megaphone replied and questions were tossed back and forth. The skipper of *The Gay Lady* or maybe Otto appeared to be satisfied for the sailboat continued on its way. But she had served her purpose by distracting the yacht crew's attention up ahead; by this time we were well in towards the stern. The searchlight made one or two more ineffectual flickers in the direction of the sail of the receding fishing boat and then went out.

Now we could hear the whine of turbines and a pump thudded monotonously. The sea swirled heavy and viscous along the hull of the yacht and we scraped alongside. I held my hand over the cat's mouth and stroked the nervous animal. Then I passed him over to Phillips. I found a chain hanging from somewhere overhead, eased up on to the rubbing strake and then grasped the ship's rail.

I slipped the knife out of its sheath, wiped the water from my eyes and looked around. Nothing was moving. Yellow light split the darkness but the foredeck was hidden from me by the superstructure. Heavy boots were resounding and I could hear the clank of a winch.

I reached down for the cat which Phillips passed up to me. He had tied a piece of webbing over its mouth which it resented greatly. I loosened this before removing it entirely and soothed the cat's ruffled feelings. Then I put it inside my shirt where it stayed reasonably still. By this time Phillips had joined me. I told him to follow and take his instructions from me. I knew the layout and he didn't. He had got his revolver out and with the knife I thought we were reasonably well equipped to tangle with trouble.

We crept forward moistly across the deck. I eased open the companion way door and we were back in that familiar corridor. The dim lights burned as before. I grasped Phillips by the arm and guided him forward. We stopped suddenly. There was a big man in the corridor wearing a black sweater and a gold-braided yachting cap. I didn't give him a chance.

" Who are you?" I said.

He looked me up and down. " Charter skipper," he said shortly.

" Police," I told him. " Keep your mouth shut and keep out of the way unless you want to lose your ticket. You got some funny people aboard."

He looked at me a moment longer and then put his hand to the peak of his cap.

" Right, squire," he said. " Thanks for the warning."

He went away about his business fairly smartly and didn't look back. I saw Phillips grinning when I glanced out of the corner of my eye.

" Lesson One," he said. " That could have been nasty handled a different way."

Then we heard footsteps coming down the corridor. I slid back the door of the skipper's cabin and we got inside. I kept the edge of the door open so I was able to stop Charley Fong before he got by. He looked at me like I was a ghost. He had tears in his eyes and his face was a nasty whitish-yellow.

" Steady, Charley," I said. " Everything's under control." He grabbed hold of me like I was one of his revered ancestors.

" So glad you come, Mlistah Faraday," he said. " Missy in great trouble. I hear her scream. Very bad business."

I grabbed him by the shoulder so hard he nearly cried out. " What are you talking about?" I said sharply.

He looked at me sadly. " They take her boss's cabin," he said. " I show you."

We went down the deck pretty fast, Phillips' revolver fanning out ready for business. But nothing stirred in the length of the corridor. Charley Fong opened the door of Mandrake's suite and snapped on the switch. We went on in.

I stopped Phillips. " Keep guard here," I whispered. " You're the only one with the gun so you're elected. If things get tough don't wait but fire."

He saw the logic of that. I went with Charley Fong through into the bedroom. I knew what to expect but it was rough just the same.

Diane Morris lay on the big master bed, her limbs sprawled out in a position which suggested she had been defending herself. She was quite naked and quite dead. Her body was covered with cuts and bruises and her arms were a mass of scratches. Her eyes were wide open and a little blood had come out of the corner of her mouth as she died.

There was a big hole over her ribs where the bullet had gone in. It was a large calibre automatic, a Luger I had no difficulty in guessing; it had been fired at close range and the flesh round the entry wound was charred and black. There was a smell of powder in the air. I put my hand on her arm. She was very cold. I should think she had been dead about three hours.

I went and got hold of a blanket from somewhere in the cabin and covered her over. I hadn't really been angry since this case started but something snapped then. Charley Fong was crying out and I let go of his arm and some of the redness went from in front of my eyes.

"I'm sorry, Charley," I said. We went into the outer cabin where Phillips was. I explained what had happened.

"Here's what I want you to do, Charley," I said. I gave him the cat. His eyes brightened.

"Wait here," he said. He went out. He was only away about three minutes. He handed me a big meat cleaver.

"Better than knife," he said simply. I thought of Otto's size and got his point. I took the cleaver gratefully and stuck it in my belt. We crouched inside the cabin door on the floor and talked. I asked Phillips to tackle the crew's quarters. He demurred at first.

"If you can bottle up the crew members in the forward mess, I can handle Otto," I said. "Mandrake's bound to be diving and that will only leave one or two men for the pump. The skipper's neutral. Charley will give me a hand. And if anything does go wrong you can still come amidships. Besides, this is personal, like I said."

Phillips looked towards the inner cabin, thought for a moment and then turned back to me.

" Let's go," he said.

The three of us went out on deck.

3

We had arranged to give Phillips ten minutes to get in position and we checked our watches again before we started. We watched him duck away among the super-structure on the shadowy side away from the diving opera-tions. When he came to the lit area he got over the rail and stood on the rubbing strake. Only his finger tips were visible on the edge of the deck and nobody would be look-ing at those.

Charley Fong followed me, carrying the cat. He was breathing heavily. I gave his shoulder a reassuring squeeze and he turned on an anaemic smile. But I knew he hated Otto so I guessed he'd do his part. We crept forward be-hind some crates and rested in the shadow while I figured out the next move. I eased forward and took in the scene on the foredeck.

A chain of floodlights blazed overhead, suspended on metal framing from the rigging. The big metal-shod boom was swung out over the port side and from it a wire-rope ladder descended into the shiny black surface of the water.

I couldn't see Mandrake anywhere around, so I imagined that I had been right; he appeared to be diving. He was using a conventional diving suit which accounted for the pumps.

There were only three men on deck that I could see. The ugly seaman and his friend, who had helped to put me in the tank, were busy turning the handles which drove the air pump. Their grumbles were audible over the steady,

rhythmic thump as the old-fashioned big metal wheels kept
turning.

The white rubber airline snaked along the deck and disappeared over the rail; it was tied across the top of one of
the wooden railed sections of the deck, just by the gangway where I'd gone over when Otto shot me. The thick
manila rope of Mandrake's lifeline drooped slackly alongside
the air pipe. Both were supported underneath by a towel tied
to the rail, to prevent chafing. The rope ran from the
barrel of a winch which was in the locked position. No-one
was working the winch and the rope was slack, like I said,
so I guessed the diver had reached the bottom.

I shot a glance at my watch. Six minutes had gone by
already and I wanted to be sure it was Mandrake on the
sea-bed before Phillips opened up. I couldn't see Otto for a
second or two; he had been hidden by a dangling boom
but he stepped out, lighting a cigarette. The light made a
cavernous mask of his face. Then he blew out the match,
flipped it over the side and stepped to the rail.

He looked quietly out over the sea and I was surprised
he didn't find my hatred corroding through the cloth of
the coat on his back. He feathered the smoke, then turned
around again, looked casually at the two seamen toiling at
the air pump and walked across midships. Just at that
instant a red light glowed and three sharp, imperative pips
sounded through a loudspeaker.

Otto stepped over to a large metal case set down on a
crate on the deck. He lifted up a hand microphone excitedly.

" Yeah," he said rather thickly.

" Otto." It was Mandrake's voice. " I have found the
buoy."

Mr. Mandrake's tones were cool and self-assured but the
effect on the three men was extraordinary. It was a moment
of high drama for them but I had to forgo the pleasure
because something else came up right then. The ten minutes

were up and the silence was broken by the single, sharp crack of a revolver somewhere up in the crew's quarters. Things then started to happen rather suddenly and the situation went rapidly out of control.

I nodded at Charley Fong and we both stepped out into the light. Charley flung the cat in a curving arc at Otto; the big man broke off his conversation suddenly and saliva dribbled out of his mouth. Charley's aim was good and Otto found a black fury clawing at his face and eyes. He gave a thin scream which mingled with the hissing of the cat and then he went over the crate backwards. One of the seamen had dropped the wheel on his side of the pump and he came up with a cannon in his hand and lead went whining across the deck.

I caught a glimpse of the other seaman doggedly pumping Mandrake's airline and then Charley Fong stumbled forward, a red stain spreading out on the front of his white housecoat. The gun boomed again and a splinter tore from the mast. By this time I was across the deck swinging the cleaver. Something split through the tail of my shirt as I passed the group round the pump and then madness was boiling in my veins.

I swung the cleaver and bounded to the rail. I sheared through the airline with one blow and it dropped overside in a shower of bubbles. I swung the cleaver again into the thick manila rope whose other end was secured round Mandrake's body on the sea bed. This was a tougher proposition and it took three chopping blows before that dropped away too.

The gun boomed again while I was doing this and a long splinter of wood screamed angrily from the deck and rained dust and debris into my face. I went tearing into the group round the pump. I guess I must have been a pretty fearsome sight for the seaman still uselessly turning the handle fled. Then I saw Charley Fong get up and come in a long rush at the seaman, who was still aiming at me; the gun flamed once more but this time Charley got him behind the knees and the shot went up among the stars.

Otto was still screaming. He rolled down the deck with the cat's small sharp teeth fastened into his windpipe. As I reached him, one of his flailing feet caught me a sharp blow across the ankles and I went down. Charley Fong and the seaman were rolling over and I heard the Chinaman groan as his shoulder hit the deck.

Ian Phillips' revolver cracked again as I got up and feet were pounding the deck in the bows. Otto flung the cat from him and got to his feet. He looked as big as a house. As he came at me across the deck, his hand swung clear and the barrel of the Luger came up. His eyes were wide open and still with the madness in them and froth dribbled down his face.

He was too late though by a mile for I had got my balance then and I brought the meat cleaver down from way over my head. It went in the top of his brain box and sheared half of his face off as it came out at his chin. Blood and brains gushed down over the blade and the light in his one remaining eye went out. He went over with a crash like a falling monolith and blood spattered the deck. The Luger slid across the planking and fell with a splash into the sea.

I went over to the seaman and put the butcher blade of the cleaver against the side of his head and tapped him into unconsciousness; Charley Fong rolled over and I helped him up. His feet buckled under him and he lay against the foot of the mast, clutching at his chest.

" You did pretty well, Charley," I told him mechanically, like I was talking to a child. I dropped the cleaver then and stood away. Ian Phillips had appeared on deck by now. He stood watching silently; the remainder of the crew came out with their hands up. The big figure of the skipper fetched up the rear with a shotgun.

I went over to the loudspeaker. It seemed like a year since I had cut the airline but it couldn't have been more than a minute in real time. I sat listening to Mandrake choking but in the end even I had had enough. I flipped the switch and turned the noises off.

I went up to Ian Phillips and asked him for a cigarette; I forgot he hadn't any. He stood quietly covering the crew. I noticed he didn't go near Otto. I went and stood up in the bows and looked at the night until the skipper came up and put a cigarette in my mouth. He lit it for me and went back to Phillips, still minding his own business.

It wasn't until I heard the siren of Clay's police boat coming across the water that I began to tremble at the knees.

Epilogue

I

I SAT with Stella and watched the sea creaming up the beach. The Catamaran seemed its usual, quiet self. The local Press boys and two agency men from Nassau had been and gone and the island was beginning to resume its seasonal lassitude. McSwayne went by along the terrace and gave me a beaming nod; the ten-day wonder had given the hotel a celebrity value that was good for business.

Mandrake's body had been recovered, my friend Barney had received recommendations for uncovering the Chicago loot and the local inquiries had duly come and gone. Doc Griffith's taste for violence had been satiated with his recent spate of post mortems. Even the prospect of the Scottish Pipe Band's visit didn't worry me any more. I put my arm round Stella's shoulder and drew her close to me.

"I'm glad we're leaving soon, Mike," she said quietly. "The routine of L.A. suits me after this holiday."

"Don't tell me you're cracking," I said mockingly.

She withdrew her body from my grasp. "You know better than that," she said. "But murder and tourism don't mix. You must admit that you brought this one in like Macbeth at the finale."

She'd got a point there. I didn't bother to reply but I was just reaching out for her can when there was a cough behind and Colonel Clay was standing there. We moved up from the pool and ordered drinks on the terrace. Colonel Clay raised his glass and we drank.

" I think I've got everything sorted out, Michael," he said. " Now that we've had your preliminary deposition we shan't need you any more, the Nassau people tell me."

" Good," I said. " Time I got back to work."

The Colonel smiled.

" Just one thing puzzles me," said Stella. " Just where were those two men taking Melissa's body when we came across them?"

The Colonel chuckled. " You won't believe this," he said. " There's an old disused graveyard up beyond the point. No-one's been buried there for more than eighty years. And no-one goes there. Our two characters had already dug a grave for Melissa. How's that for gall?"

" We should have waited," I said. " I always wanted to see a home-made funeral."

Stella shot me a disapproving glance.

" You sure you won't stay on until next week?" the Colonel asked me. " We've got the return visit of the Scottish Pipe Band and the Yacht Regatta begins on Saturday."

" I'd be sorry to miss the pipe band," I said seriously. " I'll take a rain check on it."

As Clay got up to go I said. " I still think it was a bit of a risk letting Mandrake dive for the money anyway."

The Colonel smiled. " I don't think so," he said. " You see, we'd already raised Melissa's instructions the previous night. I dived for it myself. During the engine breakdown. We put a dummy package with phoney instructions for Mandrake to find. All in all, not a bad night's work really."

I gasped for air. Then as I struggled for words, the Colonel added, " Don't bother to say it, Michael. You thought the police out here were rather slow."

He laughed. " No need to see me off."

A minute later the scarlet Alvis went past the front of the hotel and down the dusty road. I went over to the hire Cadillac which Phillips had recovered from Stanley Bay. When I came back I saw a splash of flame down by the swimming pool. A blonde girl in a scarlet bikini stood poised against the sky, then she jack-knifed down into the pool with scarcely a ripple. Stella came up to me. She put her hand through my arm without a word. We went into the hotel.

2

A few days later I went down to see Charley Fong in the General Hospital. He was doing fine. I gave him the thousand dollars Mandrake had paid me as a retainer. He wouldn't need it now and it would do Charley some good. It would just about cover his expenses and eating money back to 'Frisco. In the end I came out to get away from his gratitude.

After that I went back on up to the town graveyard. It was a small place, for whites only, and it wasn't hard to find. There was a mound of fresh-turned earth with that raw look it always has. There was a standard wreath, from a town florist, the one the municipality always provide. It's bad for the tourist trade otherwise.

I put my own small spray at the head of the grave. It wouldn't last long in this heat. I stood for a minute. It was peaceful here, though the noise of the sea could be heard just around the point. Nothing stirred and after a short while I came away.

We left the next afternoon. The Colonel came down to

the airstrip to see us off, grave and formal, but with a surprising warmth as he said good-bye. There was just him, Ian Phillips, Doc Griffith, an airline representative and the usual group of unidentified coloured folk.

We circled the strip once and I could still see his handkerchief as we passed over the field for the last time. Phillips was saluting. Stella was silent at my side and she made a pretence of craning out of the window, though there was little to see.

The pilot straightened up on course and then we were over the little cemetery, heading out to sea. I thought of Diane once again, that last night I had seen her. The island slipped astern. Summer was already going. From the air the earth looked dusty and the brightness of the flowers was beginning to fade.